Christmas
in Cardwick

By

Racquel Henry

Marabella House Books

Published by Marabella House Books.

First Edition.

Find more about Racquel and her books, please visit her website: www.racquelhenry.com.

ISBN: 978-1-959787-99-0

Cover design by Natalie Henry-Charles at Pretty Peacock Paperie
Proofreading by Jenn Lockwood Editing
Interior design by Book Obsessed Formatting

For the Unit always: Mommy, Daddy, Nat Nat, Jeffy, Ella,
Roman, and Titan

Also for Lindsey Jorgensen, Leticia Christie, and Medgine Colin

Chanel

I stood in baggage claim at the conveyor belt, searching for my gold, hard-shell suitcase, when I saw him. I was supposed to be minding my business, my eyes shifting from bag to bag as they moved in slow motion. But I looked up when I should have kept my focus on the moving belt. I took my eyes off the prize for one second, and my heart stopped. The people buzzing around the busy northeastern US airport blurred, the holiday music ceased, and everything got quiet.

The low cut.

The silken brown skin.

The dark eyes with an intensity that always turned me

into an electromagnet.

At the next conveyor belt over, and directly in my line of vision, was Greyson Reeves. Greyson Reeves, the boy who broke my heart at eighteen. The very same Greyson Reeves who knew exactly how to take my breath away.

Except, he wasn't supposed to be able to do that now—not twelve years later. Staying away from my hometown during the holiday season wasn't easy when I missed my family, but it kept me away from Christmas and, most importantly, away from Greyson. Of all the flights coming into Cardwick, his time of arrival had to match mine.

Lucky me.

He made eye contact with me, smiled, and lifted his arm to wave. I waved back, then looked away, remembering that I vowed never to fall under his spell again. I'd made a mental quit list, and he was on it—permanently. Just as I focused my attention back on the conveyor belt in front of me, the tail end of my gold suitcase disappeared behind the flaps, back to the loading area.

Great.

I let out a deep sigh, and before I could really sit in my frustration, a hand was on my shoulder.

"Chanel?" a rich, familiar voice said.

The deep inflection picked me up and catapulted me back to a version of my life I thought I had erased. My gaze lingered on the bronze hand resting on my shoulder. Maybe

I was afraid to be too close to those umber eyes again. But I snapped out of my haze and put on my armor instead.

I met Greyson's eyes with ice. "Hello, Greyson," I said, turning back to the conveyor again. He had already distracted me once—make that twice. Once, all those years ago, and just a moment ago. I wasn't about to miss my suitcase again—or let my heart get caught off guard.

"It's good to see you, Chanel," he said, leaning closer to my ear.

The familiar scent of Axe and soap filled my lungs on inhale. I used to savor it the way you would savor the aroma of your favorite dish. It was always dangerous when he was this close. I concentrated harder on the pieces of luggage moving past, the mechanical sound of the belt, the other passengers heaving their luggage off once they spotted it. Basically, anything other than the way my skin blazed under his gaze or the tingle that just shot up my spine when his lips had been *that* close to my ear. I hated that I wasn't looking at him but still felt every ounce of his presence.

"Are you back for the holidays?" I asked, still avoiding his eyes, and ignoring his comment. What was I supposed to tell him anyway? *I was hoping I'd never see you again?* Never mind how unrealistic that was in a small town like Cardwick, where 99.9 percent of the townspeople were always in your business.

"Yeah, I'll be here for a couple weeks," he said.

Fun.

The color gold flashed before my eyes, and I inched closer to the belt. I reached to grab my suitcase, but Greyson's hand grazed the side of mine, landing on the handle before mine could.

"I got it," he said and lifted it off the belt. He swung it to the side of him, and it landed with a thud between us. He chuckled—deep, mischievous, and familiar.

I rolled my eyes. "What's funny?" I folded my arms across my chest.

"I was just thinking how some things never change. You were always *own-way*, as your mother would say." His lips curled into a smile.

I fought a smile of my own and continued to be all stone. "Actually, things do change. And I'm not as headstrong as you and my mother seem to think. I just know what I want." I grabbed the handle of my suitcase. "Thanks," I said over my shoulder and took off, wheeling my bag to transportation. I needed to get out of here. It was probably twenty degrees outside, but I was burning up. I tugged at my scarf as I weaved through the crowd.

"Chanel, wait." Greyson hustled behind me, closing the space I tried to put between us.

Why won't this guy leave me alone? He had no trouble doing that years ago, so it shouldn't be an issue now. I kept walking, but of course he caught up. He walked alongside me, keeping up as I quickened my pace. He placed a hand on my arm, which set off sparks in the graveyard that was supposed to be my heart. I stopped to face him.

This time I was closer, looking at him straight on, noticing every detail of those brown eyes the same way I used to. Again that Axe and soap scent returned to the atmosphere, clouding my head and making me dizzy. He was definitely right: some things never changed. I closed my eyes and let out a deep breath while my stomach twisted.

"Is everything okay?" Greyson asked.

"Yeah, everything's fine," I said, but my words came out full throttle. They held my truth: he still made me nervous. It was my last attempt to appear like I was holding it together. We were right in the middle of a throughway, and I tried to ignore the annoyed looks people tossed our way as they maneuvered around us with their bulky coats and baggage.

"Okay," he said, but the slight worry line above his eyebrows told me otherwise. "Listen, I really meant what I said back there. It's really nice to see you. I was kind of hoping we'd run into each other. I just didn't think it'd be so soon." The corner of his mouth turned up a little.

"Well, it was bound to happen in a small town like Cardwick," I said.

"Yeah, I guess so." He adjusted the backpack on his shoulder. "You never said how long you'd be here."

My phone dinged in my coat pocket. "I'm between gigs until the start of January, so I'm here for the rest of December."

I tucked one of my dark curls behind my ear and glanced down at the message notifying me of my January interview date with Marvelwest University. I was home to see my family because I missed them, but I also had another reason—one that had to do with the interview. It was my secret, mainly because I wasn't sure what I wanted to do next. The only thing I knew was that this world-renowned flutist was tired of being on the road.

Greyson moved in closer to get my attention.

I clicked the sleep mode button on the side of my phone and pushed it back in my pocket. "Sorry."

"So, we're home together—I mean, at the same time." He shrugged his shoulders. "Maybe we can grab a coffee at Alice's Diner, catch up while you're here?"

"I don't know. My mom, aunts, and sisters are going to keep me pretty busy while I'm here." I couldn't tell him I didn't know if I could handle being around him for more than a few minutes—and alone, at that. I was standing here with him in a tiny airport where "Sleigh Ride" blasted through the speakers, and I couldn't handle it.

He deflated a little. "Yeah, of course. I mean, I knew that."

I kept trying to convince myself I shouldn't feel bad. He deserved to feel what was a fraction of the pain I felt all those years ago. But as usual, he had found his way under my skin and into my sympathy. "We'll probably run into each other, though. You know Cardwick." I shrugged and tried to sound more cheerful.

"I hope so." His eyes locked with mine.

For a second, no air could enter or leave my lungs, but I blinked and shook it off.

"I, uh, better get going. My family's expecting me any moment," I said. All I wanted to do was get over to transportation, look for my cousin Penny's car, and grab a ride out of there—fast.

"Yeah, mine, too," he said, sticking his hands in his pockets.

I offered him a weak smile before I turned on my heels and headed in the opposite direction. I tried to concentrate on how happy I'd be when I saw my family, instead of the staggered and unwelcome beats of my heart.

Not again, Greyson Reeves. Not ever again.

Greyson

I thought about her on the whole ride over to my parents' house. Chanel Baldwin. Before I saw her, I was thinking about new sheet music and technique, but now I was thinking about her golden-brown curls, and spellbinding eyes, and the way I would notice the familiar curve of her perfect lips just before I leaned in to kiss them. She was the obsession I'd sworn off when our careers had taken us in different directions. One look at her after not seeing her for twelve long years, and I was already unraveling. How was I going to make it through December?

My encounter with Chanel consumed my thoughts

even now as I stood in my parents' kitchen. Mom had gone overboard this year, and I shook my head while I took in the mini Christmas wreaths she placed on every single one of the dark-cherry cabinet doors. I reached into the giant snowman jar my mother kept on the counter and scooped out a bunch of marshmallows. It was a collectible—a gift from Chanel's mom, actually, who was also my mom's dear friend. That wasn't going to make this trip easy or less awkward, but I'd already anticipated that. I dropped the marshmallows into my hot chocolate.

"It's so good to have you home, honey," Mom said, halting my thoughts.

"I'm glad I'm not traveling for concerts this year." I brought my Iron Man cup to my lips. Chanel had given it to me one year for my birthday, and it had been my favorite ever since. I always left it here because somehow that felt safer than having it bounce around in suitcases while I was on the road. The rich, velvety liquid reached my mouth. *Mmm.* There was something special about my mother's hot chocolate.

"You sure?" Dad said, clapping my back.

I narrowed my eyes. "What makes you ask that?"

Dad rubbed his beard. "You seem a little far off, is all." He reached for the Christmas-wreath-themed teapot Mom had put the hot chocolate in.

"Something on your mind?" Mom was on the opposite side of the counter, but she reached across to give my hand a squeeze. When I glanced up from my chocolate, her shiny brown eyes were fixed on me, which meant she either already knew or had a feeling. Being on the road so much and traveling to big cities sometimes made me forget what it was like to live in a small town.

"Clearly you already know," I said, fighting a smirk.

"Alice said she saw you at the airport," Mom said.

"Here we go," Dad grumbled.

Alice Chapman was our fairy grandmother, as the town had nicknamed her on account of the fairy godmother being her favorite character from the movie *Cinderella*. She claimed that she liked to sprinkle magic wherever it was needed—just like in the movie. She also liked making homemade wreaths that she randomly sprinkled around the town every season. But really, she enjoyed meddling in everyone else's business, which was not uncommon for small-town folks in Cardwick.

"What was Alice doing at the airport?" I asked, sipping my hot chocolate. It warmed my insides and made me nostalgic.

Mom rolled her eyes and smiled. The wrinkles on the sides of her eyes expanded. "Now, you know it's the holidays. Everyone's in and out of the airport. She was dropping off Thomas's cell phone."

Dad raised his eyebrows. "Again? He's lucky he has such a patient wife."

Mom shrugged. "Seems like it's a regular thing for him as of late."

Dad stirred his chocolate. "Guess that's what happens when you start getting old."

Mom tapped him on the shoulder. "Speak for yourself."

I chuckled. I missed their banter. Traveling with the Regal World Philharmonic was what I'd always wanted to do, and I'd worked hard for it through high school and college, but it was lonely, too, especially when you had spent your whole life in a small town like Cardwick. People were always around, and the town felt like a big family.

"Anyway," Mom interrupted my thoughts, "Alice said she saw you talking to Chanel Baldwin."

"Chanel?" Dad folded his arms across his broad chest. "She's in town? Can't remember the last time she was home for Christmas."

"Is that so?" I pressed my lips together.

"Said if she didn't know better, the two of you might have traveled together." Mom raised an eyebrow and placed her hands on her hips. "There something you want to tell us?"

I almost spit out my drink, which then made me choke on it. I coughed, then cleared my throat. "Okay, this town, and everyone in it, is too nosy for their own good. She must not have witnessed the whole conversation, because Chanel Baldwin wants nothing to do with me—not anymore."

"Mmmhmm," Mom said.

I put my cup down on the counter—a little too hard because it clinked, then echoed. "It's been years, Mom. Time to let it go. I did talk to Chanel. Her plane arrived at the same time as mine. Trust me, if you heard our conversation, you would know whatever we had is very much over." My heart jolted, and my stomach flopped at those words. Of course it was over—it had been for twelve years. Still, the word *over* sliced straight through the middle of my heart. But why? It shouldn't slice anything, especially because I was the one who ended things. It was my own fault she hated me.

"Whatever you say, dear," Mom said, but her eyes were wild, which often meant she was up to something.

Dad chuckled and reached for a Christmas cookie. During Christmas, there were always cookies with extra-thick icing on the counter—in addition to all the Trinidadian sweets Mom made.

"I mean it, Mom. I'm not looking for anything serious. Not with Chanel or anyone else. I'm getting back on the road soon anyway," I said. I was due to conduct with the Regal World Philharmonic on the next leg of the tour, which was across the Caribbean. We had a pit stop in Orlando first, though.

"Well, maybe one more round of meddling for the road?" Mom said, her dark-brown eyes shining.

"What have you meddled with now?" I asked, keeping my tone serious.

She smiled wider and patted my shoulder. "I might have volunteered you for something." She pursed her lips and lightly tapped her hands together.

I let out a deep sigh. "What is it this time?" She'd done her fair share of signing me up for things I didn't necessarily want to do as a kid. Like the time she made me square dance to raise money for the Cardwick Children's Hospital. It was for a good cause, but I didn't particularly enjoy putting on cowboy boots that were too big for me, which led to me missing a dance step, which led to me face-planting onstage in front of the whole town. Chanel and my guy friends never let me live that down.

"Well, you know how important the annual Song of the Seasons Contest is to this town..."

"Mom!" The Song of the Seasons Contest was a friendly contest between Cardwick and two of the neighboring towns, Marvelwest and Ivanhoe Springs. Every year, each town chose one representative—which could be an individual, pair, or group—to write a new holiday song. They held a concert for all the townspeople to attend and charged for tickets. The ticket money was also the prize money, which the winning town could use for whatever they wanted.

My mother held up both hands. "Hear me out. Right now, our community band doesn't have a conductor because poor Lillian had to rush off to Florida. Her daughter's gone into labor! You know Lillian usually handles writing the song each year."

I pointed to myself. "What does that have to do with me? I'm not a songwriter."

"But you have more music experience than anyone else in this town. You're a renowned conductor and accomplished musician. You play multiple instruments and can carry a tune. Naturally, I said if there's anyone that can take over, it's my Grey." She beamed.

"It's not quite the same thing. And I wouldn't call myself a singer just because I can carry a tune." I closed my eyes and pinched the bridge of my nose. "I'm supposed to be taking a break. You know how much work this is going to take?" I loved my career, but all I did was work. I was tired and looking forward to slowing it down for a few weeks—something I hadn't been able to do in years.

"But you love music. And you can sing well enough. Plus, we do have another volunteer that can help you. Besides, if you don't step in, then we won't have a Christmas song this year. You know how much the contest means to everyone." Mom pouted. "And the town was going to use the money this year for the children's hospital, which needs repairs."

I locked my jaw and looked at Dad.

He shrugged. "The contest is pretty casual. It's not like you'd be prepping for one of your fancy concerts. I heard the competitors from Ivanhoe Springs aren't professional musicians at all."

Mom folded her hands together where they rested on the marble-top kitchen island. "It's all in good fun. And you could still have a few days to rest, then start next week."

Suddenly, I was back to that childhood square dance. Was I going to end up with my face plastered against the wood floors of some old auditorium again if I decided to help? She drove me mad, but I couldn't help but have a soft spot for her. What was I supposed to do? I looked down at my cup on the counter and shook my head. "Fine," I said through gritted teeth. I just needed to keep reminding myself it was for a good cause.

She wrapped her arm around my shoulders and squeezed. "I knew you'd do the right thing. It'll be fun. You'll see." Her wild gaze returned, which triggered the thought that there were missing pieces to this puzzle. What had I gotten myself into?

Chanel

"**Y**ou did what?" I said, shouting over the parang music blasting through the speakers at my parents' house. It didn't matter how many years my parents had spent in this small town, they were never going to let go of their Trinidadian traditions. Playing Trinidadian Christmas music above a normal volume was one of them. My dad continued to nod his head to the beat while I glared at my mother. All of us—my mother, two aunts, father, and cousin—were sitting on the insulated back porch overlooking the Cardwick Lake, looking at old photo albums. My aunts both lived next door, on either side of my parents. It was a childhood dream between the three sisters come to life.

Mom put back one of the baby photos of me she had just held up for everyone to see. "I don't see why it's such a big deal."

"Yeah, you probably won't even need to practice much. It's all for fun," Auntie Franny said. A strand of her short brown hair fell over the thin headband she wore.

"You're a pro at the flute already anyway," Auntie Lyndie said. She sat next to Auntie Franny, which put her platinum-blonde hair in direct contrast to Auntie Franny's brown.

My cousin, Penny, glanced at me over her glasses and shrugged.

They all thought it was so easy once you learned an instrument. But there was much more to it than that. You had to practice, practice, practice. You had to remember not to break the phrase by breathing. You had to keep the tempo and make sure you were in sync with the rest of the orchestra— not lagging or too far ahead. You had to listen while you balanced reading and playing the notes in tune. That required dedication, concentration, and again, lots of practice.

I uncrossed my legs and sat up straighter. "First, you all tell me I work too much, and the first Christmas I make it home in forever, you put me to work?"

"Where is your Christmas spirit, Chanel?" Mom took a sip of coffee, her eyes probing for an answer. "You used to love Christmas."

I studied the water. That was before. Christmas was one of the items on my quit list now. As hard as it was to not celebrate with my family, there were too many painful memories of Grey that came with Christmas, and they had no business dominating my thoughts these days. I looked away from the water, and everyone was staring at me, daring me to say no. They had all cornered me. I sighed, and they collectively leaned in closer. Except Penny, of course—she was always on my side.

"Will it get you people off my back?" I made sure to keep the aggravation in my voice.

My mother and aunts nodded—a little too eagerly if you asked me.

"I'll do it," I said, grumbling.

A group cheer rose above the music.

Dad smiled, and Penny shook her head.

"That's my girl," Dad said.

"Back to more pressing matters," Auntie Franny said, her lips curling into a mischievous smile.

"What now?" I asked. I'd just gotten here, and they were already wearing me out.

Auntie Lyndie held up a photo of Greyson and me, her red, freshly manicured nails covering the bottom corner. In the photo, we sat on this very porch, holding hands and laughing—probably at one of Grey's corny jokes. That was something I used to love about him. He always made me laugh. An aching feeling rose like a monster wave I couldn't control. This was exactly my reason for keeping my distance. My mother held onto everything, and there was no way she was going to get rid of any of her old photos, which meant when we got together as a family and often did things like this, memories I wanted to forget would always resurface.

"You really should get rid of some of these old photos." I pressed my lips together.

Auntie Lyndie tucked the photo back into the album. "Don't try to change the subject. Alice called earlier today before you arrived."

"And?" But I already knew what would come next. Where there was Alice Chapman's name, there was town gossip.

"That's my cue," Dad said, getting up from his chair. He kissed me on the forehead and opened the glass door to our family home. Once on the other side, he nodded his head to the beat of the parang music. He was probably headed for another slice of Mom's black cake.

"She said she saw you talking to Greyson Reeves," Auntie Franny said. She tried to hide her smirk by taking a sip from her coffee cup.

I scowled. "So what?" It should have been no big deal—not just for me, but for everyone. So then why had I thought about our exchange almost every minute since it happened?

"That's all you have to say? You run into your ex-boyfriend—who you only broke up with because you had different college plans, might I add—and that's all you've got? You have no thoughts on the matter?" Mom lifted an eyebrow and stared at me, telling me with her eyes that she was reading my mind. It was something I'd hated since I was a kid. Somehow, she always knew things about me before I even knew them. It was impossible to lie to her, even if I wanted to.

"Since you all are in the business of directing my life, would you like to tell me what you want me to say?" I dropped my elbows to the armrests on the chair and folded my hands over my stomach, shifting my gaze to each one of them.

Auntie Lyndie and Auntie Franny scoffed. My mother, on the other hand, rolled her eyes.

"So, you're telling me you felt nothing?" Mom raised an eyebrow full of mischief.

"Other than annoyance that our flight times matched up?" I said, my voice containing a little edge.

Mom threw both her arms up in the air. "You're insufferable. And in my opinion, there's a reason you haven't really dated anyone seriously all these years."

Auntie Franny smirked and ran her fingers through her short brown hair. "Twelve years and that heart of yours has been spoken for this whole time."

"Ya know," Auntie Lyndie said, bursting into a laugh.

Penny shook her head. "Leave her alone, y'all. If she says Greyson is in her past, then he's in her past. And who knows? Maybe Chanel will meet someone new."

I mouthed thank you to Penny. "Not likely since I'm married to the music. But for real, Penny is the only true family member I have." Well, Penny and my other cousin, Halle, who wasn't going to be flying in until Christmas Eve. The two of them always had my back.

They all laughed. As much as they were getting under my skin right now, I had to admit I missed this. My aunts had been around my whole life, and I often spent a lot of time bouncing from house to house with my cousins growing up. We had a tight-knit bond, and I made a mental note that I needed to visit them more. One thing I didn't want on my quit list was my family.

"I'm just saying, he's not like any other ex. You two didn't break up on bad terms. You broke up because you had different opportunities, and you had to follow your own paths...which might lead back to each other." Mom picked up her coffee again and took another sip.

"Mom, it's ancient history. It's just like Taylor Swift said, 'We are never, ever, getting back together.'"

"Right," Auntie Franny and Auntie Lyndie said at the same time.

The mischievous twinkle returned to Mom's eyes again. "If you say so."

Greyson

*I*t was too cold for us to play ball at our old high school court like we were used to doing on the rare occasion that all of us guys were back home at the same time, so we resorted to the Cardwick Community Center. I stopped to guzzle water while my best friends, Harland and Keston, took turns shooting free throws. Adrenaline pumped through my veins, and despite the fact that I was well out of shape, I forgot how good it felt to run up and down the court with my best friends. It was great to let off some steam. I was already dreading my first songwriting session with the other volunteer later in the evening. I had no clue what their experience level was—music wise, anyway. What if it was someone I couldn't work with? Then, there was the whole Chanel situation. No matter how much I tried, I couldn't get her out of my head. I'd only been home for about a week, and already, I was catching glimpses of her everywhere I went.

"Hello? Earth to Grey." Keston waved his hands in front of my face.

I recapped my water bottle. "Sorry, what did you say?"

Harley and Kes burst into laughter.

Something bothering you?" Harley dragged a towel over his short, curly hair.

"Or someone?" Kes asked, his lips spreading into a smug smile. He loosened his dreadlocks.

"What? No." I tried to brush them off—though it was useless. They likely had already heard about Chanel and me at the airport. Curse this town.

They both folded their arms and stared me down.

"Look, it's not a big deal. We ran into each other, exchanged a few words, and that was it." I grabbed a towel and wiped the sweat on my forehead.

"That's all?" Kes said. He folded his tattooed arms across his chest.

"Why does everyone keep asking me that?" I clenched my jaw.

"Because we all know you've never really fallen out of love with Chanel Baldwin," Harley said. He shrugged like his accusation was no big deal.

"What would even remotely give you that idea?" I asked, even though, all of a sudden, my heart picked up pace. It should have been slowing down after chasing a ball down the court.

"It's not hard math." Kes tapped my arm. "You've never been able to keep a serious girlfriend since Chanel."

"And you nitpick anytime you have a date, which is almost never," Harley said.

I opened my mouth to fight back, but then couldn't help the invasive thought that popped into my head: *They had a point.*

Kes pointed his index finger at me. "I bet you kept that ornament she gave you, too. Don't think we forgot about that. Matter fact, I bet you didn't get rid of anything she gave you."

I clamped my jaw. Chanel loved Christmas, which was always something I loved about her. One year, she gave me a round ornament that opened at the middle so you could fit something inside. She'd put a wallet-size photo of the two of us in it. It was small enough to fit in the pocket of my suit jacket, so I took it to all my concerts as a good luck charm— even for all the years we were apart. It always made me feel like she was close. Besides all that, it was perfectly normal to have a good luck charm, regardless of its history.

Harley raised an eyebrow. "We're right, aren't we?"

I shook my head. "Just because you own a bookstore and are well read, doesn't mean you know everything, Harley.

Doesn't matter anyway. She wants nothing to do with me."

The three of us pulled on our sweats over the shorts and tees we had on. That was the one drawback about winter: we were always in and out of layers.

Kes pulled his dreads out from the neck of his sweatshirt. "Have you tried talking to her? You don't have to tell her you're still in love with her right away, but maybe you can *warm* her up." He wiggled his eyebrows.

Jerk. I took a deep breath. "I'm. Not. In. Love. With. Her."

More laughter. They were starting to work my last nerve.

Harley pushed his glasses up so they rested higher on the bridge of his nose. "Look, we're just looking out for you. If you still have a thing for Chanel Baldwin, this might be your second chance."

"It might be your last chance," Kes chimed in.

I didn't say another word. I honestly didn't know what to say. Seeing Chanel confused me. I'd tried to prep myself for the moment, thinking I could handle seeing her again with ease. So much time had gone by, and she was simply a part of my past, albeit an important one. But if I was being totally honest with myself, those were lies I had used to get me through the last few years. There was something still there. But was it just old feelings because Chanel would always have a reserved spot in my heart the way old flames sometimes did? Or was it more? And did it make sense to go excavating emotions I'd already buried?

The old Cardwick Auditorium was the same, except for the fading beige walls, the worn seats, and the scratches on the music stands. I stood on the stage where our local band usually played. Our town band was much smaller than the major orchestras I'd been used to throughout my career. I turned my back to the door and faced the empty chairs onstage. Just as I began flipping through some of the band's sheet music at my podium, the auditorium door slammed shut behind me.

"It's always a good sign when your partner shows up earl—"

I'd know that voice anywhere. Chanel. Her words hung mid-air just as I spun around to face her.

"What are you doing here?" Her voice wavered.

"Getting ready to write a song. What are *you* doing here?" I should have been asking the questions. She was the one that interrupted my Zen. "A few more minutes and you might have disrupted my session."

"*Your* session?"

"Yes, *my* session. I'm writing the holiday song for the Song of the Seasons Contest." The nerve.

Her mouth hung open. "You?"

"Yes, me. Noticing a pattern here? Seriously, it can't be

that surprising, considering my backgrou—" And then it hit me. It would also make sense for Chanel to be here, too. "Wait, don't tell me you're the other volunteer."

She rolled her eyes and folded her arms across her chest. "It can't be that surprising, given my background." Her head swayed back and forth in an exaggerated motion. "And I'd hardly call it volunteering."

I had to agree with her on the volunteer part. We stared at each other like we were daring the other to blink. Then both of us said in unison, "Your mother?"

I shook my head. "Yup."

"Ugh. I'm going to kill my mother—and my aunts—when I get home." She removed the red-and-gold scarf from around her neck, then flung it onto one of the seats in a huff, along with her winter coat.

"Same. It will be the first Christmas where the paper will read: 'A Christmas Murder in Cardwick,'" I said. Now everything added up. It was already awkward enough between us at the airport. Now we'd be forced to interact because of the contest. Although, no one really needed to force me to spend time with Chanel. I'd do that without any coaxing if she wanted to. She stepped directly in front of one of the stage lights, and the memories of us road-tripping the summer before college flashed in my mind. I could still smell her gardenia perfume, see the wind charging through her curls, feel her ocean-soaked skin as I pulled her in for a kiss at the beach.

"Grey? Hello?"

Her voice snapped me out of the trance. She now stood closer to the stage, looking up at me and snapping her fingers.

"Sorry. I was just—"

She waited, her eyes still and laser-focused.

"Nothing. What were you saying?" I turned back around as she went to the stairs at the side of the stage and made her way up.

"I was asking if you had anything in mind this year?" she said.

I flipped through the scores on my podium. "I was just looking through these for some inspiration. I'm thinking something half dreamy, half romantic. Something like 'Merry Christmas, Darling' meets 'Christmas Dreaming'?"

"I like that. Aim for the heartstrings. Those are two of my favorites." Chanel took a few steps to where I was standing at the podium and leaned in. She was close, and her being this close to me sent a spark through my whole body. I took a deep breath, which only made things worse because she smelled like vanilla and roses. It made me dizzy and nostalgic for all the times we'd sit on her parents' back porch. We'd sit in the quiet, holding hands and looking out at the water.

"We're on the same page," I said. At least about music anyway. I watched her as she studied music scores. So much was different and the same. Her once long curls were a little shorter and stopped just under her shoulder blades. Every feature on her face had become more radiant, and it wasn't from a physical standpoint. She had grown not only as a musician, but as a woman. A woman who could still halt my heart.

She turned a page and smiled. I tilted my head to the side so I could see what she was looking at.

"'Merry Christmas, Baby,'" I said.

She kept her eyes on the page. "You remember this?"

My heart lurched in my chest. "Of course I do. We practiced that flute and piano duet for months. My mom still says that's the best Christmas gift she ever got."

"My parents said the same. Who knew a Christmas concert present from two nutty teenagers would go over so well? It made the time spent worth it." She still didn't look at me.

"I wouldn't have cared if they liked it or not. The time spent with you was always worth it to me." I should have thought a little harder before saying that, but it just...came out.

This time, she looked up from the music, her gaze shifting to me. Neither one of us said a thing and just searched each other's eyes. I didn't know what we were looking for, but my eyes dropped to her lips, and it felt like the most natural thing in the world. It felt like this was twelve years ago, and she was still mine. That was, until she snapped me out of it. She took a step back, and she was right there, but that subtle bit of distance made me miss her. I missed being close to her and was tempted to erase the distance she put between us, but I gave her the space she obviously wanted.

"Um, so I guess we should maybe do some brainstorming on our own and meet up for another session? We only have roughly a week." She tucked a curl behind her ear, a nervous habit of hers I always loved. "What's your schedule like?"

"I'm pretty free outside of family Christmas stuff. I was really supposed to be relaxing, so I hadn't planned much."

"Same. My first holiday break in years, and my mother insists I work." She shook her head.

"Right? I figured touring kept you busy, but before I got back, I didn't know you hadn't been home for the holidays."

She shifted her weight from one foot to the other. "Yeah. It was better for me to be on the road, working. I stopped celebrating Christmas years ago, and going home meant that I'd have to." She pressed her lips together.

She met my eyes, and my chest ached. Like me, she had stayed away from Cardwick during the holidays. Christmastime used to be special for us, until I ruined it by telling her we should cool things during winter break of our freshman year of college. I didn't blame her for not wanting to celebrate it. I hadn't wanted to either, hence my decision to say yes to every Christmas gig I was offered. It didn't help that our families were always together either. Not facing things was easier, and it won every time.

Two things dawned on me then. One, I was an idiot. And

two, all I wanted for Christmas was a second chance to right this wrong.

"I get that." I wanted to tell her I broke my own heart, too. We let another few moments of silence pass, and I said, "Maybe we can each brainstorm on our own tonight and then meet up tomorrow night? My family wants me around for Christmas activities tomorrow, but I'm free in the evening."

"Me too. Sounds like a plan," she said, taking the side stairs to the stage. She grabbed her coat and swung it over her shoulders. I wished she could have stayed so we could catch up, but I took some comfort in the fact that I'd see her tomorrow. "See you tomorrow, partner," she said.

I cracked a smile. "See you tomorrow, partner."

I didn't know how to fix this, but maybe I could figure it out. We were going to be spending a lot of time together over the next week, and maybe it was my chance. But did I want to fix it? Even if I did, what then? I was due in Orlando next, then I'd be traveling the Caribbean. And she likely already had her next gig location as well. When we were younger, I didn't know how to make a long-distance relationship work, but I hadn't even given it a shot—nor did I give Chanel one. I could cross that bridge when and if we got there. For now, I needed to at least *try* to get her to want to try again.

Chanel

*A*fter a two-and-a-half-hour flute practice session, I tapped my pencil against my notebook while I sat on a bench in Cardwick Square. I'd promised Penny we could go Christmas shopping, but this song had to be written. I figured what better place to write a Christmas song than the heart of Cardwick, where garland curled around every light post, wreaths adorned every shop door, and colorful lights were strung on every surface. I had a few ideas but not much to work with. Staring out at all the Christmas decorations that covered every inch of Cardwick's main hub, I willed words to appear. When they didn't, I closed my eyes. Maybe they'd appear behind the dark of my eyelids. I could carry a tune, and I'd written a few songs before for fun, including one for a project during music school, but it wasn't exactly where my strengths lay. Give me some sheet music and the flute, and I could make those sing. Make me write a song, and I was mediocre at best.

The bench shook, and then there was a thud. Penny.

"How's the brainstorming going?"

I kept my eyes closed and didn't move. "How does it *look* like it's going?"

"Looks like you're on a roll," she said.

I finally opened my eyes and glanced at her next to me. She didn't even try to hide her smirk. She adjusted her gingerbread-themed scarf.

I stretched. "You want to write this for me? I would gladly pass my volunteer duties over to you."

"Nice try." She stood up. "Let's walk and talk. We don't have much time until we have to be at your parents' house."

"But you're the writer in the family," I said, getting up and falling in stride beside her.

"Yeah—of fiction." She stopped to admire the jewelry in the window of Judy's Jewels. "And it's not like I'm a professional. I'm a hobbyist."

I held out both my hands, palms up. "Tomato, tomaaato. And you *choose* to call yourself a hobbyist. Your writing is good."

We continued walking. "I think I'll stick to books. You're

the musical genius. Besides, the only reason you really want out is because you have to work with Grey."

I rolled my eyes. I'd texted her and my other cousin, Halle, the second I got out of my first session with Greyson last night. They hadn't been much help, though, since both of them thought it might be fate at work. They were wrong. Once something made it on my quit list, there was no turning back.

"Greyson Reeves is ancient history," I said.

"Except, he's not. You're writing a song with him for a town contest. That would make him a current event."

I shrugged. "Fine. Call him a current event, but we will not be repeating history. I know my history very well, so I'm not doomed to repeat it."

She gave me the side-eye. "Mmhmm."

I smacked her arm, and she laughed.

"So, how's Harley?" I asked, putting her in the hot seat now.

Penny blushed, then said, "He's good. I just got back from switching shifts with him at the bookstore."

Harland was Penny's best friend who owned Cardwick's only bookstore, Basket of Books. They'd been best friends since elementary school and were also madly in love with each other, though neither one of them wanted to admit it. The whole town had been waiting for them to confess their feelings for years.

"I need to stop in and pick up a few things. I want to take

some books back with me to read while I'm on the road." I paused. "One day, I hope I'll be able to grab the latest Penny Persad from his store."

"You might be waiting a while. Writing careers take time," Penny said.

"You girls getting all your shopping done early?" a voice said behind us.

We stopped and turned around to find Alice Chapman wearing a Santa hat. Three wreaths with sparkly red-and-gold ribbon were draped on one of her arms.

I smiled. As meddlesome as she was, she was adorable. "Hey, Alice. We're trying to."

She leaned in, the corner of her mouth turned up. "Heard you and Grey were gonna be representing the town in the Song of the Seasons Contest."

As if she didn't know. I nodded. "You heard right."

Her eyes shimmered. "Uh-huh. I'm quite happy to hear it. You two have always been so talented. And who knows what else might come of it."

I wrinkled my brows.

"You know, opportunities, dear." She smiled so wide it reached the corners of both of her ears. "And if you decide to get Grey a Christmas present—"

"Thank you, Alice, but I'm not big on Christmas anymore, so I don't think that will be necessary." It was the politest way I could think of to shut this conversation down before it went too far. Once upon a time, shopping for Grey was my favorite Christmas activity. Everyone wanted me to *remember, remember, remember,* but it was going to send me spinning out of control. I'd already done that once when Greyson and I ended things.

Penny cleared her throat. "You know what? We're actually running out of time and need to head out for dinner. Better get going. Right, Chanel?"

"Right," I said.

Alice shifted her weight and offered a curious expression. "It's good to have you home, Chanel." She moved past us and hustled down the sidewalk.

The front door slammed behind us as we entered my parents' home. Mom and Dad stood in the kitchen, shopping bags spread out across the glittery white countertops. The sweet smell of stew filled the air.

Mom stirred her pot. "Hey, girls."

"Hey," Penny and I both said.

"I'm making a quick cook. A pot of stew chicken and red beans with rice for you, Chanel. Everyone, including the Reeves family, will be here in less than thirty minutes," Mom said.

I swiped a Christmas cookie from Mom's Santa jar. "Do

the Reeveses have to come over? Trimming the tree is our tradition. Better yet, let's skip the tree this year."

"Stop it. You know Charlotte's one of my dearest friends, and we always include them in our celebrations. They're practically family, too. Plus, you and Grey have to work on that song, so we might as well have them over."

It was bad enough that I had to spend time with Grey on my Christmas break, but now he was infringing on time with my family, too—although I had suspected I couldn't avoid that. And it wasn't like I was thrilled about all these Christmas activities. It was starting to feel like there was no safe zone.

I glanced at Penny, who cringed.

In a short time, Greyson would walk through my family's door. Now, what should have been a relaxing family event would turn into an event spent on guard.

Dad brought the last box of Christmas decorations in from the garage and placed it in the living room near the bare tree. As much I loved when the whole house smelled of pine from a live tree, we'd been using fake trees for years. One holiday season in college, my roommates and I decided to bring a live tree home—pretty typical thing to do at Christmas. Except, along with the tree came a stowaway squirrel. In. The. Tree. Which meant that it was also in our apartment. The story ended after we found said squirrel under one of my roommate's bed and had to call a few close guy friends to remove it. A half hour later, it eventually ran out the window. I still remember all the loud banging that rung in my ears. After that trauma, I never wanted to see another live tree again.

The doorbell rang, yanking me from my college years right back to the present. My heart rate quickened. My aunts and their families were already here, so we were just waiting on the Reeves family.

I heard the latch of the door release, and my mother's voice. "Hi, Reeves family! Come in, come in." There was laughter and excitement as Mr. and Mrs. Reeves greeted my mom.

And then I heard his mellow voice. The one that used to calm me down in a second flat. The one that always managed to send a shiver bolting down my spine. It annoyed me that his voice had any effect on me at all. It shouldn't. I used to compare his voice to all the things that made me feel comfort, like Sunday mornings. Pancakes. Sunsets. Now, there was only one thing it made me feel: anxious.

That anxious feeling heightened when Grey rounded the corner, and our eyes immediately locked. It took me three seconds to realize what I was doing before I shook it off and stood up.

Mrs. Reeves appeared right behind him, her salt-and-pepper hair held in place with a shiny red hair clip. "Let me look at you, Chanel," Mrs. Reeves said, placing two hands on my shoulders. "You've certainly gotten more beautiful." She glanced back at Grey. "Wouldn't you say so, Grey?"

My cheeks heated, and I imagined that scene in the latest Spiderman movie with all the sand, the one where it was alive and made things disappear. I needed something like that at this very moment.

"I'd have to agree with you, Mom."

My eyes shot up at that. And again, it was like he had some kind of hidden magnet. Nope. I wasn't going to let Greyson Reeves draw me in again just because he said something nice. There was a reason he made it on the quit list.

My father entered the room, carrying a cup of hot chocolate in his hand. It was his favorite drink, even outside of the holidays, so it was a solid bet it could be found near him. "Hey! Glad you all could make it."

Mom clapped. "I think we can get started on the tree. Reeves family, can I get you all something to drink? Maybe some ponche de crème?"

"That sounds great," Mr. Reeves said.

My stomach churned, but maybe the spiked holiday drink would do me some good.

The Reeves family greeted my aunts, uncle, and cousin, while Mom went to the kitchen to pour the drinks.

Dad turned on the parang music and grabbed a string of lights. Baron's "It's Christmas" filled the air, and as Mom came back with the tray of drinks, Dad pulled her in for a dance. That prompted Greyson's parents to get up and dance. My attention slipped to Grey, who was already looking at me. My heart skipped. We had so many memories of the two of us dancing to parang music right here in this living room. My eyes stung as images of us holding each other close flashed before me like ghosts. I had to get out of here. I swiped a glass off the tray my mother had brought in and headed for the back porch. Fresh air. That was what I needed.

I opened the sliding door and almost regretted my decision immediately. I'd forgotten to grab my coat, and it was freezing. Although the porch was enclosed, it was all glass, and the heating was off. Plus, it was always colder near the water. Too late now. I'd just stay out for as long as I could stand it. I sat down on one of the chairs. Was I going to get through the next week? It'd been twelve years. But everywhere I looked, those ghost memories of me and Greyson kept showing up. *Even on this porch*, I thought bitterly as I took a sip of my drink and looked out at the water.

I heard the whoosh of the sliding door behind me. Greyson appeared next to me, holding out the plaid throw blanket from our couch.

"Thought you could use this," he said, a frosty cloud escaping from his lips.

Lips I used to kiss.

Do. Not. Go. There. Chanel.

I took the blanket and wrapped it over my shoulders. Much better. Why did he have to be so considerate? "Thanks," I said.

"Saw you roadrunner out of there. No time for coats with that kind of speed." He chuckled.

"You saw that, huh? I just needed some air. Too much Christmas in there and too much…"

"Me?" he finished my sentence.

Years ago, I would have been thrilled for us to be out here alone. Now, I was nervous for some reason. I glanced down at the drink in his hands. "You like it?"

"Yeah. Forgot how good it was. I haven't had it in years," he said.

"Same," I said.

Grey took a seat on one of the chairs across from me and leaned back. "Been a while since I sat out here."

I nodded and gulped my drink, kept my eyes on the milky liquid in the glass.

"Wonder how long it would add up to if we calculated how much time we spent out here," he said.

Something tightened in my chest. "Probably years. In the spring and summer, we even did our homework out here." I did my best to push those images of us away.

The awkwardness hung between us for a few beats, both of us searching the water. The sun had just gone down, and the sky was a muted blue.

He opened his mouth to say something, then closed it and waited. Finally, he said, "Look, I know this is awkward... and maybe a little intense."

"You think?" I found it hard to keep my anger in check. I could feel where this was going.

"Chanel, I know I hurt y—"

"Don't." I bolted out of my seat. Those words. He hadn't used many, but those words...*I* and *hurt* and *you*. They were like a lancet to the skin right before the drip of blood. "Don't talk about it. You don't know anything about how I felt. You weren't there. Your name is on my quit list in permanent ink, and that's where you're gonna stay."

I almost apologized when I saw the affliction in his eyes.

"Wait, you have a list?"

I folded my arms. "Yes, I have a list. Some people have bucket lists...I have a quit list. It's everything I'm not going back to."

He nodded. "Understood."

I let out a deep breath and concentrated on controlling my tone. "We have a lot of work to do with the song. Let's just try to get through it."

"Okay," he said, his voice depleted.

I thought I would want to hurt him the way he hurt me, but the way he was looking at me made me want to reverse everything and run straight into his arms. Life didn't work like that, though. You couldn't wave a wand and undo things.

Instead, I turned my back and went inside. Nothing was worse than the realization that no matter what I did, he seemed to always influence my emotions. I'd never go down that road again. I could talk to him. I could even write a song with him. But I would not be taking any trips down memory lane with him. Greyson Reeves was never going to have the chance to break my heart again.

Greyson

W hile everyone went paranging around the neighborhood, Chanel and I hung back to work on our song. Most Trinidadians thought going door to door singing Christmas songs and picking up others along the way was fun, but it was too cold for it. According to our families, though, nothing could stop a good time, not even the weather. Never before had I been happier to have a commitment. Besides that, I got to be alone with Chanel.

Although I loved being around her, I also had a hard time shaking the feeling that my heart had capsized and gone under. Our porch conversation earlier had gone left—and quick. Did I even have another shot with her, or was it in vain?

"Grey?" Chanel said.

"Hmm?" I said, my thoughts all dissipating.

"I asked if you liked the title?"

"Sorry, what was it again?" I needed to make a conscious effort to focus.

"'The Christmas I Found You.'" She glanced up from her notebook, and a loose curl slid above one of her eyes. She didn't even know how beautiful she was.

Somehow, I'd managed to contribute despite the welcomed distraction. We'd written the hook and spent a little time practicing it. I pretended to need a better look at the title she'd scribbled and leaned close to her. "I love it." I pointed to the title on the page, and my hand brushed hers. It was a true accident, but you wouldn't have been able to tell my heart that the way it carried on against my ribcage.

She sucked in a breath, then turned her attention back to the notebook and twirled the pencil between her fingers. It was the most attractive thing, the way her eyebrows creased just a little when she was concentrating. I loved watching her think.

She stopped twirling the pencil and folded her arms. "I love it, too. I feel like it really sets the tone. The title and the lyrics can be romantic, and the melody can have that dreamy vibe we're going for."

"We'll probably win," I said through a yawn.

Chanel smirked. "Am I boring you?"

I stretched. "Never."

She blushed but tried to look away so I wouldn't see.

"So, you got everything all sorted out for your next gig?" I asked.

"Yeah. We're going to be in Vermont next."

"Vermont in January. Sounds...cold," I said.

"It's not any colder than Cardwick," she said, shrugging.

"This is true."

She tilted her head to the side. "What about you? Where you headed?"

"Orlando."

"Nice and warm," she said.

"Yeah. Although, I heard they have cold weather. It's just not consistent," I said.

"Still, there's sunshine." She stood up and twisted her torso in a stretch. "I think we deserve a reward. Mom made black cake. Want some?"

"No one could resist your mom's black cake."

I followed her to the kitchen. It took everything in me not to pull her close when she reached in the cupboard for the dessert plates and her red hoodie hiked up, revealing a sliver of smooth, brown skin. She set the porcelain Christmas tree plates down, then opened the lid on the butter cookie tin her mother used to bake the cake in. The sugary smell filled the air as soon as the slice was on the plate, and again, it made me nostalgic for the time we were together. "How many times did we sit at this kitchen island and lick the bowl? Or steal a bit of whatever your mom was making?"

She let out a laugh. "Mom hated when we stuck our hands in her batter."

"That was half the fun. I'm just glad she didn't send me packing for being a bad influence on you."

She held out a fork for me and held my gaze. "She would never. She really loved you, Grey. She still does. She and Dad always felt like you fit right in."

I swallowed and didn't take my eyes off hers. Her mother might still love me, but did Chanel?

She blinked and nodded to the slice of cake. "Dig in."

I reached for it, and she came around the other side of the island to stand next to me. I had to pull my eyes away from her mouth as she took her first bite. I stuck the fork in my own slice and tasted. "This should be illegal," I said through chews. "Your mom's still got it."

"She's the best Christmas baker I know."

"Same. But don't tell my mom," I said.

"Secret's safe with me." She smiled, which triggered a wildfire across my whole chest. It almost knocked me over. I missed her smile, and I missed being the one that made her do so.

"How do you like playing with the Globe Orchestra?" I asked.

She put her fork down for a second and leaned on the island. "It's nice. Everyone's great, and it took me a while to find my groove, but once I did, I really felt comfortable."

"But something in your voice doesn't sound like it's a total love fest." I took another bite of cake.

She sighed. "I love my career. But..." She paused and bit her lip. "But it's also hard being on the road all the time."

I shook my head. "I know what you mean. You're surrounded by lots of people—a whole orchestra's worth—but it's still lonely."

"You get it. And after so many years of doing it, you just realize something's missing. And you don't exactly know what. Sometimes I think about what would have happened if I stayed in Cardwick, you know? Would I feel more...settled?"

"You were always bigger than Cardwick. You had to take that path. You're an exceptional flutist, Chanel."

She offered a warm smile. "So are you—an exceptional conductor, that is. And you're not bad at all those other instruments either. I guess we were both bigger than Cardwick."

Something flashed in her eyes, and I could tell she was thinking about the twelve-years-ago version of us.

"I know what you mean, though—about feeling like something's missing."

We held each other's gaze, which I realized we were doing a lot of lately. She was holding a lot of anger for me, maybe frustration and sadness, too. But I wondered if she still felt a fraction of what I was feeling, even though her words indicated otherwise. The "something missing" for me had always been her. I just wanted what was best for her, but the second I'd ended things, I'd never been whole again. I wanted to tell her that, but she would probably shut me down again. She didn't trust me, and honestly, I didn't blame her.

I don't know what made me do it, but I looked up, which made Chanel look up, too. Along with the ornaments on ribbons her mother had hung from the ceiling, was a ball of mistletoe. Right above the two of us. Again, our eyes connected. I knew I shouldn't have, but I took a step toward her, closing the distance between us, then reached out and placed a hand on her hip. She took a small step back, and for a second, I thought she might slap my hand away, but she didn't stop me.

My heart was beating out of control in my chest, and so was hers, based on the rise and fall of it. I moved my gaze to her lips, and she did the same.

"I can't do this," she said, breathless. She kept her focus on my lips and leaned in.

Following her lead, I leaned in, too, then slowly ran my thumb back and forth along her jawline.

But a key jingled in the lock at the front door. As everyone's voices and laughter filled the house, she backed away. The desire that was just all over her face disappeared, and she replaced it with the stoic look she'd been giving me since we had set sights on each other at the airport. My heart plummeted.

"Hey, you two." My mother's voice filled the space first. She entered the kitchen, and so did the rest of our families.

Mrs. Baldwin pulled off her knit hat. "How's the songwriting coming?"

Chanel cleared her throat. "Good. We, um…got the title and the hook done."

Mrs. Baldwin glanced down at our plates, then up above my head, and exchanged a look with my mom. I knew what they were thinking. And honestly, I wished it were true. I wished Chanel and I had kissed. And I wished she'd let me in again. But I was also starting to wonder if it was a pipe dream.

Mrs. Baldwin pointed to our plates. "I see you all tried my black cake. What do you think, Grey?"

"It was delicious. Definitely one of the things I missed— among other things." I looked at Chanel when I said the last part. She only let me have a second, then busied herself with grabbing our plates and putting them in the sink.

My mom's thin lips spread into a smile. "Well, I'm glad you two got some work done. And I can't wait to hear that song. It's pretty late, though. You ready to go, Grey?"

"Yeah. I'll meet you outside. Chanel and I need to figure out our next meeting time." When Trinis got together, there was often an extended gathering outside when it was time to leave. Somehow, they managed to get into other conversations while saying their goodbyes—didn't matter the weather.

Mom went over to Chanel and squeezed her shoulder. "Okay. It was so nice to see you, Chanel. We might see you all again for New Year's Eve."

"Nice seeing you again, too, Mrs. Reeves," Chanel said, giving my mom a hug. Lucky her.

As our two mothers left the kitchen, the energy in the room only intensified. I rubbed the back of my neck. "Um, so...should we talk about—"

"Grey."

How could she switch so easily from almost kissing me to icing me out? Maybe I was just setting myself up for another heartbreak. Maybe I'd lost her forever. If I had, it was my own stupid fault.

She clearly didn't want to talk about what just happened—or almost happened—so I said, "I was just going to ask what time we should meet tomorrow. In the evening again?"

"Yeah, that's good for me."

"I'll text you in the afternoon, then, so we can decide where," I said.

"You still have my number?"

"Of course I do. I wouldn't just delete something that meant so much to me," I said, backing out of the kitchen. She didn't say anything else as I made my way to the front of the house and put on my coat. Opening the door, I wrapped my scarf a little tighter once I felt the gust of frigid air. It was extra cold tonight.

"You never deleted her number?" Harley asked, stuffing a waffle into his mouth. We'd just finished a basketball game at the gym, and I was anxious to get to Alice's Diner, owned by our town fairy godmother herself. I wanted to eat here as often as I could before I left. It was one of the few places you could eat out and it still tasted homemade. There just weren't very many places like that on the road.

I poured some syrup over my pancakes and eggs. "Why is that so hard to believe?"

Harley smirked. "It's not. But I knew it."

I shot him a menacing look.

"Not deleting her number is an indication you never got over her, which is exactly what Kes and I tried to tell you the other day." He gulped his orange juice.

"I *was* over her," I grumbled. "I just stumbled into the Chanel vortex again."

"Dude, you were never out of it. You've been spiraling for years. And for the record, I don't think you're going to get out. Her winds got you *caught*."

"I had moved on. I was living my best life on the road, you know." Never mind how the road sometimes felt lonely.

It was still my wildest dream achieved.

"Keep denying it, man."

"Let's say that's true. Like I've been saying, none of it matters. She's moved on. She told me I was on her quit list—in permanent ink."

Harley laughed. "That's...deep. Then again, so is the wound. Have you told her what you're feeling?"

"She won't let me. She's basically shut me down at every attempt—not that there have been a ton."

"Ouch."

"That all you got? I need some help here."

"She doesn't trust you. You're going to have to figure out how to earn that trust back. You need to remind her of how much you loved her—and still do—while also assuring her that you're not gonna break her heart again."

"No sweat." When he put it like that, it felt more impossible.

Harley took another gulp of orange juice to wash down his pancakes. "As you know, I'm no expert in this department. I've been trying to tell my best friend that I'm in love with her since we were in grade school. But I think you need to stop putting so much pressure on things. Write the song with her. Try to have fun. I think, deep down, she's still in love with you, and if she is, she'll come around."

"Maybe." I cut into another pancake. "Think you're ever going to tell Penny how you feel? Maybe take your own advice?"

Harley shook his head. "I don't know. I want to. But I don't want to ruin our friendship if things don't work out."

"Harley, you've been able to maintain a friendship for years. There's no reason you can't make it work romantically. The chemistry is real. Everyone's seen it. Maybe something else is holding you back."

"It's complicated. But what I do know is that if I lost her as a friend, I don't know what I'd do."

"I get it. But if you take too long—and you've already taken too long—someone else might swoop in," I said.

He paused his chewing, then swallowed. "I know."

"Look at us. We have no idea what we're doing," I joked.

"Do any of us?"

No. I didn't believe any of us did.

Chanel

I held the final note of the piece I was practicing a little longer than necessary. Once it finished vibrating through the air, I kept still. It was what we liked to do onstage, too. You held still for a few beats, keeping the audience in suspense. It was just long enough to pull a little more out of the moment. Enough to catch your breath after being hypnotized by the music. My parents were out at the Cardwick Gingerbread House Contest. I'd helped Mom put the finishing touches on her entry while she subtly tried to grill me on Greyson.

He'd been on my mind too much lately, especially after

that nearly kiss. And then he had to go and tell me he never deleted my number. I had never deleted his either. But it wasn't because there were any feelings left. I kept all my contacts, and I needed to know if he contacted me so I could ignore it.

My phone buzzed on the dresser.

Grey: Evening! You eat yet?

Chanel: No. Just got done practicing. Was about to see what leftovers we have in the fridge.

Grey: Nah. Forget leftovers. I cooked. Want to come over and work here?

Chanel: Depends

Grey: On?

Chanel: What you cooked.

Grey: You'll have to come over to find out. ☺

Chanel: What are you up to?

Grey: Don't think so much. We gotta work, and you gotta eat!

Chanel: Fine. But it better not be another attempt to get me back under the mistletoe.

Grey: Would things go differently a second time around?

Chanel: NO

Grey: I'll aim for the third time, then ☺

Chanel: ::rolls eyes::

I checked my reflection in the rearview mirror as I switched off the car in Grey's driveway. What was I doing? I rested my head against the steering wheel and sighed. I was strong. I could handle working with my ex. So what if I'd been caught up in nostalgia and almost kissed him. Even if I had, it would have just been a kiss. People kissed all the time, and it meant nothing.

I forced myself to straighten up, then exited the car. I almost lost my nerve to approach the door when I laid eyes on his parents' house. This was exactly why I didn't come home at Christmas. It was a constant reminder of my best times with Grey. Each time I'd come home over the last few years, it was for very brief periods. A weekend here. Three days there. My trips were so short that I only had time to visit my family, and all I really had to do was bounce from house to house. I didn't see much of anyone else, and I made it a point to keep a low profile. This trip, on the other hand, was too full of history and the two things I'd sworn off: Greyson and Christmas.

I stepped onto their front porch and froze when I saw the seat-swing we spent so many lazy days and nights on. Just like we had our spot at my parents' house, we had our spot here, too. I had the urge to turn around and run, but then the door opened, and Grey stood in the archway.

"Surveillance system dinged when you pulled up," he said.

"Right," I said, pulling my coat tighter across my body.

He smiled and stepped to the side. "Come in."

I tried not to make contact, but my arm touched his chest as I moved past him, and just the little bit of contact made me burn up, even through all that clothing. I undid my scarf and pulled off my coat.

And then I saw it.

The table with the poinsettia tablecloth.

The dim overhead lighting.

The Christmas lights used to frame the two chairs.

And the dish of food in the middle.

I turned to look at Grey and fell right into his chest. My weight knocked him off balance, so he wrapped his arms around my waist to steady us both. I paused, trying to regain my composure. My heart raced on, though. Finally, I got enough courage to look up at him.

"A good catch," he said, his voice deep and low.

I let out a breath and stepped out of his grip.

"Yeah. Um, thanks." My eyes landed on the table again. "What's all this?"

He held my shoulders and gently pushed me over to the table. "This is much better than sitting at a plain table," he said.

"Grey. I told you—"

"I know what you said. Can't two friends just have a nice dinner together?"

"Are we friends?" I asked, folding my arms. "And we're

supposed to be working on our song."

"Didn't we start as friends?"

"That was before you—" But I stopped myself. I couldn't go down this road without splitting myself wide open. That part of me was stitched closed. "You know what? Let's just eat and get to work. I don't want to be on the road too late."

He dropped his shoulders, then held out my chair. "Okay."

I sat and took a deep breath, straightened my back. I just had to get through writing this song. It wasn't that long we had to work together. Besides, I survived twelve years without him, and my life was fine. It still was.

He sat across from me and uncovered one of the lids.

I gasped. "No. I don't believe it."

He pushed out his chest, his smile growing wider. "And they're vegetarian friendly."

"You made this?" I stared at the meat pies wrapped in flawlessly green banana leaves. "I expected you to remember my favorite dishes, but I didn't expect you to make them."

He opened a napkin. "I had a little help from Mom, but I did most of the work." He paused for a second. "I wanted to cook for you."

He was making it hard not to remember the Greyson I fell in love with back then—the one I didn't want to think about. I also didn't want to look at him, so I reached for a pastelle instead and unwrapped the steamed banana leaf. I took a bite and closed my eyes as I tasted the perfect combination of cornmeal and veggie meat. "This is amazing," I said. I took another bite.

"I'm glad you like it."

"I'm impressed."

He cleared his throat. "It was always one of your favorite things to eat around the holidays."

"One good thing about being home has been all this food." I had to shut that comment down before it led us down another memory, which would lead to striking yet another nerve. We had work to do tonight.

"I'm loading up while I can. The food on the road is a mixed bag."

"Agreed. Sometimes it's straight-up crap," I said. A lot of the time, it could get very hectic with rehearsals, too. Often, I only had time to grab a protein bar or shake. And it depended on where you were. Some places just didn't have very many options. Grey took a bite of his pastelle, and I had to summon my willpower to tear my eyes away from his mouth. I was not supposed to be watching his mouth. He smiled, and I wondered if he'd caught me. I forced myself to look at my own plate.

"Did you bring any new ideas with you for the song?" he asked.

"I did. You?"

"I got a few."

I sat back and patted my stomach. "That was so good.

Maybe we should get started before I eat all of them."

He laughed. "Have as many as you want. I made them just for you."

I fought a smile so hard. But no matter how hard I tried, I couldn't.

I had sprawled out on my stomach by the Christmas tree in Grey's living room. We'd been at the songwriting for two and a half hours and were making good progress. We finished the first and second verses, then practiced fitting the pieces together.

Grey stretched his legs. "I don't know about you, but I could use some hot chocolate. You?"

It was tempting, but I said, "I should probably get going."

"Come on, one cup before you go? It'll warm you up..."

I thought for a second.

"Stay," he said, his eyes pinning mine.

I narrowed my eyes. "Okay, but just one cup."

He hopped up. "Deal."

I sat up and looked over what we had and hummed the melody, tweaking a word or two here and there.

"You have such a sweet voice," Grey said, handing me a cup overflowing with marshmallows. He sat down next to me, our backs leaning against the couch. His shoulder grazed mine, and like earlier, I had to work hard to catch my breath.

I brought it to my lips, then paused when a marshmallow touched them.

"Don't worry. They're all vegetarian friendly. No gelatin," he said.

Something unlocked in me that made me feel like my head was losing another battle with my heart. They'd been at war this whole trip. "You remembered."

"I remember everything about you, Chanel."

I could feel his eyes on me, but I let my cup have all my attention. I took a sip. "Mmm. That's good."

"It's the marshmallows," he said.

"Is it even really hot chocolate without the marshmallows?"

Both of us laughed, then sat in the quiet for a bit. It scared me that none of it felt awkward.

"You ever think you'll move back to Cardwick?" he asked.

I concentrated on the Christmas tree and took my time answering. "Honestly? I think about it all the time."

He nodded. "Me too."

"Really?" I asked.

"Yeah. Like I said before, the road gets lonely. But I also think I'm just getting tired. Traveling for so many years wears you out."

"It does. And once you reach a certain level of success, it gets kind of old. I've thought about teaching. I taught a few independent workshops, and I actually liked it. I could possibly get a teaching gig a little closer to home. I wouldn't mind being near my family again. I miss them." *Did I say that out loud?*

"Teaching is great. Or you could get a gig with a local orchestra."

"That's an option, too. But I actually have an interview with Marvelwest University. They're looking for a music director. It's at the beginning of January, right before I hit the road. All I know is, I'm getting the urge for a more permanent home." I hadn't even told my family, but Grey had a way of making me spill my secrets. He was always my safe place.

"Me too." He paused. "That's a big step with the interview. The music director title would look good on you."

"We'll see. I haven't told anyone about it because I don't want to get anyone's hopes up. Plus, I wasn't sure I could be in Cardwick full-time, you know?"

He stared into his cup and nodded. "I do."

"Do you think you'll ever make the leap and come back home?" I was afraid of that answer and couldn't look at him.

"I want to. Don't get me wrong, I'm tired, but it's also all I've known for so long. I struggle to just...do it. Making a change after getting my dream career seems...scary. But maybe. I wouldn't mind running my own music school one day."

"You totally could, Grey." I touched his hand on instinct but then pulled away quickly. "Are these the same two people who were so set on traveling the world with international orchestras?"

He chuckled. "I hear change is good."

"I heard something like that, too."

He paused. "If you settled down in Cardwick, does that include getting married one day?"

I shook my head. "I'd have to fall in love first."

He turned his body toward me. "And you don't want to fall in love? I mean, again?"

"I wrote love off a long time ago," I said, refusing to look at him even though he was looking at me. "Once it's on my quit list, that's a wrap."

But he ran a finger along my jawline and gently pulled my face toward him. "Sometimes you have to cross things off your list—maybe even write a new one." He brushed his thumb against my cheek, the same way he had when we almost kissed. "Besides, you not falling in love again would be a shame."

My heart drummed in my chest. "It would?" I whispered.

He nodded and switched his focus to my lips. He inched closer until there was only a sliver of space between us. Alarm bells went off in my head, but I didn't stop him.

And then his lips brushed against mine. There was only one thing I wanted: *more*. As if reading my mind, he pressed his lips to mine and intensified the kiss, heat spreading through me like wildfire. It was like nothing had changed, and when he gripped my waist and pulled me closer, I felt safe, the way I always had when I was with him. I wrapped my arms around his broad shoulders and held him tighter. It was like neither one of us could get close enough.

And then I remembered. I pulled away as both our chests heaved up and down. "I'm sorry, I—I can't do this, Grey."

"Chanel—"

Without another word, I jumped to my feet and raced to the front of the house. Grey followed me. I could hear his footsteps trying to keep up. I swiped my coat off one of the hooks his parents kept for visitors and threw it on.

"Chanel, can we please just talk about this?"

But I couldn't talk to him, couldn't look at him. My eyes were already stinging. It was more proof that he didn't understand just how much he'd hurt me. And now my walls couldn't protect me because they were in shambles at my feet. I needed out of here. I flung the door open and dashed to my car. He followed me out, but he didn't go past the front porch. I fumbled with my keys for a second, but I managed to get inside. And as I backed out of the driveway and my headlights lit up his face, I had to work hard to ignore his bewildered expression. Greyson Reeves had pulled me back in, and I couldn't drive away fast enough.

Greyson

I missed her. I rubbed my bloodshot eyes, hoping the cold air would help me look a little more alive. It had been less than twenty-four hours since Chanel stormed out of my parents' house, and I hadn't heard from her since. I hardly slept, thinking about her. I tried texting. I was actually pretty worried when I saw how frantic she was while she was reversing out of the driveway. I wanted to know if she'd made it home safely. Luckily, it wasn't that late, so I called Mrs. Baldwin, who confirmed Chanel arrived home but went straight to bed. This morning I had tried again, but that text went unanswered as well.

I didn't just miss her after last night. I missed *being* with her. And I wasn't just talking about romance between us— though, that was a big part of it. She was my best friend, and it didn't matter that we'd been separated for twelve years. I used to share everything with her. And now that I was getting to be in close proximity with her after all those years, I regretted ever letting her go. I thought I was doing what was best for her. Nothing was a bigger punch in the gut than realizing I'd made such an epic mistake.

"You're awfully quiet this morning," my father said.

I kicked the snow we'd been crunching through on our walk around the neighborhood. I needed to get some air and clear my head, so when I said I was going for a walk this morning, Dad said he'd join me for some father-son bonding. We used to do this all the time when I was growing up, but now I couldn't remember the last time we did. The few times I had come home over the last few years, time was always limited. "Guess I got a lot on my mind."

"With music, or is this about a certain woman?"

"Both."

I glanced in his direction, and he raised an eyebrow. "Oh?"

I stayed quiet, stewing in my own misery.

"You wanna talk about it?"

"Not sure there's a point, Dad."

"Try me."

"I kissed Chanel last night." I clenched my jaw.

"I'm guessing by your crappy mood that it didn't turn out the way you wanted?"

I shook my head. "It started out great. I thought I might actually be winning her back..."

"But?"

"But then she jumped up, said she couldn't do it, and ran out of the house."

My father scoffed.

"What?" I asked, not sure I was ready to hear what he had to say. He was a straight shooter, and I couldn't think of a time where he'd ever sugar-coated something he had to say to me.

"You think you're winning her back after one kiss? Come on, son. A woman like Chanel? You were the one that ended things with her, remember? You're gonna have to work a lot harder than that to win her back."

I stayed quiet, taking my anger out on the snow by kicking more of it as I walked. "I just..."

"Want things to go back to the way they were?"

I exhaled. "Yeah."

"Son, let me tell you something, things aren't going to go back to the way they were. You two have been apart for twelve years. You're different people. You can build something new, something better, but trying to look at this like you're reclaiming something old is going to get you nowhere. The old is what scares Chanel, because you let her down. You need to present her with something new—the new man you are now. The one who isn't going to let her down," he said.

We walked in silence for a bit.

"Why do you always have to be right about everything?" I said at last.

"One, I'm your father. And two, I was a young man once."

I stopped walking and squared my shoulders in his direction. "Mom?"

"Yup. I was a knucklehead at first, too. Guess it runs in the blood. We didn't have a perfect start. Your mom even dated another guy during the time we split."

"How'd you get her back?" I asked.

"I took the advice I just gave you. I worked hard—you know your mom didn't make it easy on me—and I went about building a better love story than the one we had."

I chuckled.

"What are you laughing at?"

"Just picturing Mom putting you to work."

He laughed. "You're in the same boat, so I wouldn't be pointing any fingers if I were you."

"Good point. But still." I continued to laugh.

He put a hand on my shoulder. "If you want something bad enough, you'll figure out a way. And Chanel would be a great daughter-in-law. You know your mother is quite fond of her."

I shot him a look.

He held up two hands. "Just sayin'."

I nodded. I wanted that, too, but first I had to figure out how I was supposed to do that when she wouldn't even talk to me.

After my walk with Dad, we'd gone back to the house for breakfast with Mom, after which I sent Chanel yet another text.

Grey: *You okay? I really want to talk to you.*

Figured I'd go with the direct approach. I was tired of playing games, and after all the time we had spent apart, neither of us had time to waste. I'd been sitting in the recliner with a stack of scores on my lap, studying them and thinking about the style I wanted the orchestra to use when I got to Orlando. I bolted upright and almost knocked the stack of music off my lap when I saw the three little text bubbles moving across the screen, which I'd intentionally kept unlocked. But then they faded, just like my hope that she was finally going to say something. I'd wait for her forever if that was what it took, but that didn't mean it also wasn't pure torture.

I groaned out loud. I just needed her to hear me out at least once. Then my phone dinged.

Chanel: *Okay.*

I let out a deep breath.

Grey: *Where and when?*

Chanel: *Cardwick Park Square? They have those outdoor heaters near all the benches.*

Grey: *Meet you there in an hour?*

Chanel: *Yeah.*

Now to get my head straight.

I got to the park early. I'd stopped for Chanel's favorite holiday drink from Harley's bookstore cafe—the sugar cookie latte. It was freezing outside, but we could always sit in the car with the heat on if the outdoor heaters weren't enough. Only when she pulled up did I realize how shot my nerves were. This might have been my only chance to explain things, not that I really could explain breaking up with her. Last chance aside, I at least owed her an apology.

She opened her car door and took her time getting out.

I got out of mine, too. "Hey," I said, extending the latte to her.

"Hey," she said, shivering. "What's this?"

"Sugar cookie latte—if that's still your favorite. Thought we could use something warm while we're out here in the cold."

She hesitated, then her features softened. "Thanks, Grey." She took a sip and stuck her other gloved hand in her coat pocket.

"Wanna sit?" I nodded to a bench up ahead.

"Okay," she said.

We both sat down and didn't say anything for a while. The iced trees were so still, a direct contrast to the way my heart pumped in my chest. I was glad it was so cold. Right now, I hardly felt it thanks to my nerves—and the heater, of course. I didn't quite know where to start, but I knew it was up to me.

"How you doing?" I asked.

"How do you think, Grey?" But it wasn't sarcastic. Her voice was full of pain or maybe confusion? Maybe both.

"I'm sorry," I said.

Her head turned in my direction. "For kissing me last night?"

I shook my head. "No. I'm not sorry for kissing you. In fact, I want to kiss you again and again...and again."

She took a deep breath. "You can't just say things like that unless you mean it. And you can't just kiss me *that way* when you're not sure of what you want."

"Who says I'm not sure?"

She opened her mouth to say something, then closed it.

"What I'm trying to tell you is that I'm genuinely sorry for hurting you, Chanel. I thought I was doing the right thing when I called things off all those years ago."

"For who?" she asked, folding her arms. "Me? Or you?"

"For you," I said, caught off guard.

"No, Grey. You did it for you. You didn't think you could make it long distance. You were scared, and you've always hated change. It was going to be a change for both of us—one that might not have worked out. And you didn't even give me a choice in the matter, after all we'd been through." Her voice cracked on the last sentence.

I was quiet. She had a point about me not giving her any options. "You're right. It was very one-sided of me. I should have talked it out with you. But you were thinking about giving up a spot at a top institution to move closer to me. I couldn't stand it if I stood in the way of something great for you. You're not only an amazing woman, but you're also an amazing flutist, Chanel. I wanted us to both follow our dreams."

"I guess that's the difference between us. You were part of my dream. I was okay adjusting my dream so we could both get what we wanted. I never planned on giving up my professional goal. What you showed me was that you weren't willing to meet me halfway. And isn't that what relationships are all about?"

"Trust me, I see that now, but for what it's worth, I never stopped thinking about you."

Her eyes grew wide. Was she really that surprised?

"I constantly wondered if you were seeing someone else. Whether or not it was serious. If you still liked pastelles and half a cup of marshmallows in your hot chocolate, and sugar cookie lattes. I thought about you erasing me and replacing me with someone else. And I know you'll have a hard time believing me, but that almost killed me. I never—" I paused and stared out at the snow-covered trees in the distance. "I never stopped loving you."

She didn't say a thing. Didn't move. Didn't even look like she was breathing. But I let the silence stretch between us because I didn't want to rush this. She needed whatever time she needed to process what I just confessed.

And then, she reached for my hand and interlaced her fingers with mine. My only regret was that we were both wearing gloves. My heart kicked up all the same, though.

"I never stopped loving you either, Grey," she whispered, the fog from the cold air curling around the words she just spoke.

Her words took the wind clear out of my lungs. She still loved me.

I brushed a curl out of her eyes and held her face in both my hands. Finally, she was looking back at me without shielding her desire. I eased my lips down to hers, pausing to savor every second of this moment. At last, my lips connected with hers. Her kissing me back made me think I didn't need anything else for Christmas. She was the only woman I wanted to kiss—even in whatever afterlife there was.

She pulled away. "But how are we going to make this work? We're both going our separate ways again at the end of this trip. What's going to be different this time?"

"What's different is that I am never letting you go ever again. And we're going to write a new love story. We'll make it work. We can see each other on off times, and there's video chat, and text messages. We'll figure it out."

She looked down and bit her bottom lip, which caused a flutter to run through me.

She met my gaze again. "Are you sure?"

"Never been more sure about anything."

"If we do this, you're gonna have to earn back my trust. I'm not crossing your name off my quit list until you prove you shouldn't be on there. And I have to go slow, okay?"

I kissed her hand and then her cheek. "Okay."

She rested her head on my shoulder, and we stayed like that until the sun dissolved in the sky.

Chanel

"**H**old on. Let me get this straight. You're back together?" Penny blinked and stared at me with her mouth hanging open.

Auntie Franny grinned. "I knew it!"

"Especially since Alice Chapman saw you two at the park yesterday," Auntie Lyndie said. She had a grin as wide as Auntie Franny's.

"And she said you two looked pretty cozy," Auntie Franny said. She wiggled her eyebrows.

"It was just a matter of time." My mother, on the other hand, sat casually in one of the living room chairs and took a bite of black cake.

I groaned. "I don't want you all getting your hopes up. Greyson and I just came to an agreement. He's not in the clear yet."

Penny let out a frustrated breath. "Are you back together or not?"

"We're...trying to work things out."

They all erupted in squeals and laughter. I tried to fight a smile but couldn't. I loved and missed my family— the people who just wanted what was best for me. Being around them during the holidays was pushing me in a new direction—one that terrified me. The director position with Marvelwest was becoming more appealing every minute I spent on this trip. But was I ready to give up traveling the world and be rooted in a place that maybe I'd always belonged? Still, even if things didn't work out with Greyson a second time, Cardwick was my home.

"So, tell us what went down at the park," Penny said.

I filled them in on all the things Greyson said and the promises he'd made, how we said we'd take things slow this time.

"I've always loved Greyson and thought he fit right in with our family," Mom said.

"Not that you're biased, considering one of your best friends happens to be his mom." I rolled my eyes at my mother.

"Matters not. He's always been respectful and treated you right, which is the most important thing to your father and me."

"And no one's complaining about him in the looks department," Auntie Franny said.

Another outburst of laughter.

"Seriously, y'all?" I shook my head.

Auntie Lyndie shrugged. "We have eyes."

"How's the town song coming?" Mom asked, finishing her last piece of cake.

"It's coming. We still have the bridge to do, which we'll do tonight after the Christmas festival. We've been practicing while we write, but we'll definitely need to practice everything when it's complete."

"I can't wait. And your father is really looking forward to it, too," Mom said.

"Please don't add more pressure, Mom."

She held up two hands. "We're not. Win or lose, we're happy that you and Grey stepped up to help out."

I was, too.

The Cardwick Christmas Festival had always been one of my favorite traditions as a kid, so when I stepped onto the old Cardwick Acres Tree Farm where it was held, it was like I was ten years old again. Plus, Grey and I had a lot of memories here—another reason why I had stayed away. Greyson reached for my hand as I closed my eyes and inhaled the strong scent of pine like a thick blanket in the air.

"Lots of you-and-me history throughout this whole place, huh?" he said.

I smiled and squeezed his hand.

Someone tapped my shoulder. When I turned my head to the other side, Alice smiled up at me, a bundle of Christmas lights in her arms. She wore bright-red lipstick, her signature, and her gray hear was piled into a bun on the top of her head.

"Hi, Alice," I said, glancing down at the lights. "Can we give you a hand with those?"

"I thought you'd never ask," she said, but instead of handing the lights to me, she shoved them against Grey's chest.

"Oof," Grey said just as she did. "I got it."

I stifled a laugh.

"Let's let the gentleman handle it," she said, winking at me. "We can walk and talk." She hooked her arm with mine, and Grey followed close behind us.

"Word on the street is that you and Grey are back together." She glanced over her shoulder at Grey, who just smiled.

I remained quiet, though I struggled to keep a straight face as we moved through the crowd of people participating in various Christmas activities and fun.

"Cat got your tongue?" she asked.

This time, I glanced back at Grey. He shrugged.

I tucked away one of my loose curls. "I think we've both agreed that we're working on it. How's that?"

"Call it whatever you want, but you can't fight destiny. This whole town knew it was only a matter of time before the two of you reconnected. Besides, I've worked too hard—" She pressed her lips together.

"You what?" I asked, tilting my head to the side.

"Nothing. How's the town song coming?" she asked.

I narrowed my eyes at her. Again, I was reminded about small-town life and everyone finding a way into your business. Now I was one hundred percent sure she was up to something—or at least had been.

"We're actually going to work on the bridge tonight. That's the last piece of the puzzle."

"Excellent, excellent. I have no doubt you two are going to make sure we win. You know we need that money for the children's hospital repairs."

I nodded.

"Ah, here we are," she said.

We stood in front of a stand that read: Alice's Diner. Some of the staff were already behind it, laying out all the Christmas baked goods. My mouth watered as I inhaled the mouthwatering scent of the pies, cakes, cookies, and breads—all of them decorated ornately for the holiday season.

"Wow, Alice, this stuff all looks amazing," I said.

"Slice of my famous Christmas spice pie is yours if you all help me string these lights," she said, a sly smile spreading across her lips. "My lights went out unexpectedly, and Mr.

Chapman had to run back to the bakery for all the items I forgot." She chuckled.

Both Grey and I laughed.

"I got this," Grey said. He was already reaching for the dead lights, and I went to help him. Once we were done with the lights and stuffing ourselves full of pie, we decided to walk it off.

Grey reached for my hand again, and I tried to suppress the fluttering in my stomach that the simple gesture awakened.

"Alice is something else," he said as we walked around the tree farm.

I nodded and laughed. "But at least she makes good pie."

"She does. And nice wreaths." He paused and looked ahead at the giant red barn, which held an indoor carousel. "Remember that?" he asked.

I blushed. "Our first kiss."

"And you were so afraid your parents would walk in and see us kissing in one of the double seats." He laughed.

I swatted his arm. "They could have! Besides, as much as I liked it, you know I'm a private person."

"I do know. And I love that." He squeezed my hand. "Wanna take a ride with me?"

I hesitated but then nodded my head yes.

We let go of each other only long enough to find our favorite double seat, and then Grey laced his fingers through mine again. There weren't a ton of people because there were so many other activities going on across the tree farm. Mostly, kids took up the spots on the painted horses with a few adults sprinkled between to supervise.

As we began to take off, Grey said, "There's something I've been wanting to ask you."

The fingers of his free hand tapped against his knee.

I gave his hand a squeeze. "Okay?"

"I know you usually spend Christmas with your family, and I'd never dream of taking you away from that, but do you think you'd want to spend some time with me? Christmas evening, after everything."

He finally met my gaze and brushed his thumb across mine. It sent a chill up my spine.

I grinned. "Do you have something in mind?"

"Maybe."

"What?"

He smiled. "You'll see if you say yes."

"I don't know, I'm pretty busy," I teased.

"You're really getting a kick out of torturing me, aren't you?" he asked.

I batted my eyes and pressed a kiss to his neck. "Is that what I'm doing?"

He sucked in a breath. "Listen."

This time, I let out a much longer laugh.

"You gonna answer my question or not?" His lips expanded to an impish smile.

I let all the playfulness fade from my tone and intensified my gaze. "Of course I want to see you on Christmas, Grey."

He ran his hand across his forehead in a dramatic motion. "Phew! For a second there, I thought I was going to have to pull a Ryan-Gosling-Ferris-wheel moment like in *The Notebook*. I was getting ready to climb to the top of this carousel."

I gasped, but he put his arms around me and pulled me closer. I could get used to this.

Greyson

*C*hanel wrote down the final lyric, tossed her pencil down on her notepad, and threw her arms in the air. Good grief, she was beautiful. We'd been sitting on the floor of her parents' den for the last few hours, trying to hammer out the bridge.

"Fin!" she shouted.

I frowned.

"Why do you look like someone just told you your dog died?" she asked.

"Well, we're done writing."

"Yeah…" She narrowed her eyes.

"Together. That means we're not writing a song together anymore."

"Good thing we don't need an excuse to spend time together anymore," she said, inching closer to me. She kissed me on the cheek, and I gently pushed one of her curls behind her ear. I stared into her eyes, trying to somehow freeze this moment. Now that I could touch her anytime I wanted, I didn't want to lose her. Because I'd been so stupid before, I fully grasped that I could, indeed, mess things up again.

"Talk to me. Something wrong?" she asked.

I should have known I couldn't hide much from her. But I didn't want her to know I was afraid of losing her. She was already hesitant as it was. "I just want to remember everything about this Christmas," I said.

She smiled. "Well, that's easy." She hopped up and went over to the coffee table and picked up her phone.

"A selfie?" I asked.

"Yes. But also, a new memory captured." She pressed up against my left side and put her head on my shoulder. She was made to fit there.

I put my arm around her and held her close.

"Say *music*," she said, her smile growing wide.

"Music," I said, and she pushed the button on her phone. She didn't move for a few seconds after, which was just fine with me.

"Let's see how it turned out," she said, flipping to where

the pictures on her phone were stored. Soon, the photo of us filled her screen. "It's cute," she said, studying it. She looked over at me. "Do you like it?"

"I love it." I liked anything she was a part of. I couldn't care less how I looked in the photo, but she was glowing. Another thing I wanted to remember. "Send it to me?"

She hit a few buttons, and then my phone dinged. "Done."

I took out my phone to look, and there was the photo in my text messages along with a red heart. But there was another text I hadn't seen while we were working. It was from the Regal World Philharmonic manager. I had no idea what it said, and yet my stomach flip-flopped from just the sight of the name. There was usually only one reason the manager would be trying to contact me on a break. I pushed the thought away. Whatever it was, I didn't want to deal with it in front of Chanel. Maybe I was just jumping to conclusions.

Chanel stood up. "Want to take a snack break and then run through the whole song a few times?"

"Sounds like a plan." I got up and clicked my phone off, forgetting about that text message and knowing full well I was still going to have to deal with it later.

After I left Chanel's house, I drove straight home. While we polished off what must have been the millionth piece of her mother's black cake and practiced, I'd been trying to pretend that text message didn't exist—key word being *try*. As much as I pretended, it was in the back of my mind, nagging at me. And it relentlessly turned my stomach when I thought about having to open it up and read it.

"Good evening, Grey. Song all done?" Mom asked when I entered the front door. She and Dad were sitting by the Christmas tree, drinking her famous hot chocolate, a throw draped over their legs. The fire blazed in front of them and warmed the room.

"All done." I stuck my hands in my coat pocket.

Dad held his cup up in a toast and nodded. "Well done, son."

I attempted a smile but was pretty sure I was unsuccessful.

Mom tilted her head to one side. "Everything okay?" Like Chanel, she was good at knowing when something was off with me.

"Yeah, fine," I said, turning to head back outside on the front porch. "I'm just gonna sit outside for a few minutes. I didn't feel like explaining things, and I needed to be alone when I read that text.

Mom kept her attention laser-focused on me. "Don't stay out there too long."

I stepped out and sat on the swing chair. The air was crisp against my face and much colder now that the sun had gone down. I took out my phone and held it in my palm for a few minutes, working myself up for what I was about to read.

Wishing I could just delete the text, I opened my messages and clicked on Barbara's name. Just as my gut had warned me earlier, Barbara was asking me to get to Orlando early. My stand-in conductor had hurt his arm, and they needed me to do the Christmas performance. I sat back on the swing, pointed my head to the sky, and closed my eyes. If this had happened right when I first arrived to Cardwick, it wouldn't have been a big deal, but now—now that everything had changed—I had a real problem on my hands.

Now, I was going to have to explain things to people. Now, I was going to have to explain things to Chanel. Now, I was going to have to tell her that I was being summoned back the day after tomorrow, the same day we were supposed to perform in the Song of the Seasons Contest. That meant our Christmas plans were going to be canceled, too. And it was me who made the plan. All she would see was me letting her down again. I let out a frustrated breath and placed my head in my palms. As I'd feared, here I was again, about to mess things up.

Chanel

*A*fter a quick flute practice session, I met up with Penny for a catch-up at Basket of Books. She was working the afternoon shift, so we made it work by hanging out there so we wouldn't have to cut our time too short. We'd grabbed two coffees from the cafe and now sat in two comfy chairs near the shop window, which was decked out with a gorgeous pine garland intertwined with Christmas lights. At the center was a wreath with glittering red ornaments that was Alice's handiwork. I took in the welcomed smell of new books. Although I wasn't a big reader before, being on the road had opened my time up for reading, and now I read around two or three books a week.

Harley made his way over to us. "Good to have you back in town," he said as I stood to give him a hug. With the busyness of the holiday season, he wasn't able to say hi when we first arrived. I was glad to see the bookstore doing so well—and Cardwick, too.

"Surprisingly, it's good to be home," I said. If you would have asked me that question last week when I arrived, I would have had a very different response.

Harley shot me a look, like he knew I'd changed my mind and who had changed it, then smiled. "Sometimes, coming home is the thing we didn't know we needed."

"Maybe," I said as he shifted his attention to Penny.

When he looked at her, his gaze softened. "Thanks for picking up the longer shift today. My cousins are coming in tonight, and Mom needs help getting everything ready. It's the first Christmas without Dad."

Penny placed an arm on his toned bicep and gave it a sympathetic squeeze. His body reacted with an almost unnoticeable shiver. "I'm sure she's glad she has you around."

I nodded. "I'm sorry it's a difficult Christmas, Harley."

"Thanks. We'll be okay. I just want to help her with what I can. I can't take away the fact that she'll miss him, but if I can lessen her load, then that's something." He let out a deep breath and stared into Penny's eyes one more time. "I'll let you two talk. I see a customer that might need my help. See you ladies later."

He disappeared between the shelves.

"Halle is going to make it by tomorrow for the Song of the Seasons Contest, right?" Penny asked as we both plopped back down into our comfy chairs.

"That's the plan. She's cutting it close."

"When is she not? She's done it a few Christmases. I'm just happy she can make it."

We both got quiet at the realization that I hadn't really been around to witness that. Of course I remembered Halle cutting it close from our group chat, but it was a reminder that I'd been absent from holiday festivities for a lot of years.

"Sorry," Penny said, her lips pulling into a tight, straight line.

"No, no. Don't be. It was my choice to stay away during Christmas." And it was. But it didn't calm the guilt already simmering low in my stomach.

"Hopefully, she and Kes won't be at each other's throats when they run into each other," Penny said, lightening the mood.

"I've been waiting since we were teenagers for the two of them to squash whatever beef they have, but at this point, I don't think that's going to happen."

We both laughed.

"So, what's up with you and Grey? I'm curious now after your text last night," Penny said, steering us away from the subject.

I told her about how off Grey was last night.

"You sure you're not just reading too much into it?" She smirked and glanced at the endless shelves of books surrounding us. "No pun intended."

I half-smiled. "He's been a little hard to read. Probably because we've been separated for so long. We've both changed, you know. But also, I've played with his kind of fire before, and it's not fun getting burned. Part of me is afraid he's gonna do it again."

"I get that. But you made the decision to give Grey another shot, right?"

I nodded.

"Then you have to let go. If you hold onto all that hurt you experienced in the past, you're not going to be able to really move on with the relationship. It's like you're always going to be stuck in a black hole."

I thought about that and bit the side of my cheek while my mind replayed the shared moments between Grey and me.

Penny took a sip of her pumpkin spice latte. "I see those wheels turning."

"I know you're right. I'm just wondering if maybe I was too hasty. Like, what if I thought I could do this, and I can't? What if I just got caught up in old feelings?" The knot in my stomach wasn't much help to my indecisiveness.

"I can't answer that for you. Only you can answer that. But for what it's worth, I've seen the two of you together, and there's something special there. No one can predict the future, you know."

I sank down further into the chair. "You mean crystal balls aren't real?"

She grinned. "Well, who knows? I think all you can do is take the chance. And like I said, there are no guarantees about anything, so you might as well take the risk."

"You an expert on love now or something?" I teased.

Penny threw her head back and laughed. "Definitely not an expert. I mean, look at my situation." She glanced over at Harley.

"You know, every time I've looked up throughout our conversation, he's been gawking at you," I said, a coy smile forming on my face.

Penny rubbed her cheeks. "He has not!"

"Oh, he absolutely has. You keep talking about how it's clear that Grey and I have something special, but I'd make the same claim about you and Harley."

"It's different with me and Harley," she said.

"How so?"

"There's too much history of friendship. Even if he felt the same way—which I have no idea if he does—then we might still mess up the friendship we have now."

"Pe-nny. That friendship could get messed up either way."

She furrowed her brows. "I know. But—"

"What was it you were just telling me about guarantees

and risks?"

She threw a crumpled napkin at me.

I laughed. "I want to see you happy, too, you know."

She smiled.

Now, if I could only figure out what happiness meant for myself.

I arrived to the Cardwick Auditorium early. Once inside, I flipped on the lights and threw my coat on one of the theater chairs. Grey would be here any minute. I took a seat on the edge of the stage, letting my feet dangle above the floor. Although we were supposed to be practicing and getting ready to sing our song in front of hundreds of people tomorrow, the idea of being around him made me more nervous than being in front of a crowd. I had no idea butterflies could resurrect themselves. I felt like a teenager, which was ridiculous. I was a grown woman with an established career that would take me away again soon. I should have been concentrating on the new music I'd be playing on the next leg of the tour, not thinking about when I'd get to kiss Grey again.

The door to the auditorium creaked open, then shut with a thud. Those butterflies went into a frenzy.

"Hey," Grey said as he walked down one of the aisles to meet me at the front. He undid his scarf and took off his coat.

I couldn't help but suck in a breath at the sight of his biceps under a fitted thermal shirt.

I swallowed and cleared my throat. "Hey," I said, trying to keep my voice steady.

He leaned in and kissed my cheek. More fluttering.

Until it stopped.

I could feel his energy, and I knew, just by observing the slight droop of his shoulders, that something was wrong. He took a seat next to me on the stage, and his leg brushed against mine. I ignored the tingle that zipped down spine.

"How was your morning?" he asked.

"Good. I got a nice practice session in this morning and then caught up with Penny," I said.

"Nice," he answered.

Another sign things were off. He always had short answers anytime they were. "Something wrong?"

He looked at me, and instead of wings fluttering, I felt a stab of something familiar. A gutting of sorts, like the time he suggested we break up.

He pursed his lips, like he was physically willing himself to keep something inside. "Dance with me?"

I was not expecting that. "There's no music," I said.

"We're musicians. We'll make the music." He hopped off the stage and held his hand out to me.

I tilted my head to the side and narrowed my eyes.

"Please?" he said, his voice deep but with just the right

amount of soft.

I couldn't resist him twelve years ago, and I couldn't resist him now. I took his hand and slid off the stage. He took his time pulling me close to him, wrapping his arms around my waist. I melted into his embrace and draped my arms around his neck while those butterflies threw a party inside of me. Every weird feeling I'd had a second ago dissolved, and now it was just me and Grey—and the spark between us as he held me close.

He stared into my eyes like he was trying to freeze-frame the moment. "Let's take it from the top."

I furrowed my brows. "Take what from the top?"

"You came here to practice, right?"

"Our song?"

He chuckled. "Yes. Our song. I'll start." He hummed the melody and began singing a cappella, nodding his head at me to join in.

Once I did, he held me tighter, and I rested my head against his chest while we swayed to the rhythm of our voices and the intoxicating words we created together. As we danced, my skin grew warmer, every inch of it charged from being this close to Grey. When we finished the song, he leaned his forehead against mine, his soft breath tickling my cheek and disrupting the peace in my heart. We both kept our eyes closed. I'd never felt more in sync with him.

He brought his lips to my forehead, trailing kisses along

the side of my face, then to my jawline, until finally his lips covered mine. It was slow and tender the way our lips moved together, like neither one of us wanted to break this moment. Like everything about it was fragile. He once again took his time pulling back. This time, when our eyes met, something was different about his—like an old wound you just remembered.

I ran my fingers over the back of his head. "What is it?"

He let out a deep breath. "I have to tell you something."

The butterflies collapsed into the hole that opened up in my stomach.

"Before I say what I'm about to say, I need you to know... that I'm in love with you."

My heart skipped. I wanted to say something, but everything in my brain vanished.

"I need you to know it."

At last, words started coming back. "You're scaring me, Grey, because it sounds like there's a but."

He swallowed. "I got a text yesterday from the orchestra manager."

"Sounds pretty standard..."

"They want me there early. There's been an injury, and they need me for the Christmas concert."

I dropped my arms from around his neck and took a step back. "How early?" I asked, although I already knew the answer.

"Tomorrow early."

"Grey," I said, my voice near a shout.

"I know."

"Tomorrow, as in the day of our Song of the Seasons Contest?"

He nodded.

"Huh." My voice dripped with sarcasm. "I should have known."

"You don't need me. You can perform the song by yourself, and it would be just as good—maybe better."

"That's not the point, Greyson. Of course I can handle it on my own. I've been on my own for the last twelve years. But we were supposed to do this together. And the fact that you can be so casual..." I threw my arms in the air.

"Chanel, please. It's not casual. With that kind of notice, I'm the only one experienced enough to take over." He tried to take a step closer, but I backed away and headed for the seat where I'd tossed my coat earlier.

"Your career that you said felt like something was missing. I thought that something was m—" I stopped myself before I went there. "And what about our Christmas plans?"

He was quiet, didn't even look at me. Just buried his hands deep in his pockets, his shoulders hanging low.

"You still don't get it, after all this time. You're always going to put your career before us, aren't you?" I was dizzy from the realization, the bottom of my gut splitting into the sink hole that would swallow every part of me.

"Come on, Chanel. You know that's not true. I lo—"

"Don't. Don't you dare say it. It's not just your career. You're still afraid of change." My eyes burned, and the room that was once spacious felt too small for me. "I need to get out of here."

"Chanel, don't go."

"I don't want to hear anything else. Good luck with the next leg of your tour. Goodbye, Greyson."

My heart squeezed in my chest as I pushed through the auditorium doors. It was so cold out. Finally, I felt the weather, and it seeped inside of me, icing everything over. Good. There was a reason Greyson Reeves was on my quit list. I never should have trusted him.

Greyson

I blew it. My heart had crashed, and now it was like there was a full-blown power outage inside of me. Everything was dark. I didn't blame Chanel for not understanding, but part of me had hoped she would.

"Dude, you look like your boss called you into the office and fired you," Kes said. He sat across from me in a booth at Alice's. Judging from the side-eyes everyone gave me when I walked in, I was willing to bet word had already spread about me backing out of the Song of the Seasons Contest.

"I did get fired," I grumbled, replaying the look in Chanel's eyes just before she stormed out of the auditorium last night.

I probably should have been at home, packing, but here I was, miserable and trying to down a piece of apple pie. Kes had wanted to grab a bite before I went off to the airport.

Kes cleared his throat. "You just gonna keep poking your fork in that pie?"

"Not all that hungry, I guess." I set my fork down, but it slipped out of my hand, clanking against my plate.

Everyone got quiet and turned their attention to me. I sank down in my seat. I was already dealing with the weird energy in the room, and now I had everyone's attention—again.

Alice sauntered up to our table. She wore a gingerbread-themed apron over an ugly Christmas sweater. When she stopped at our table, she raised an eyebrow over her cat-eye glasses and said, "Everything alright over here, Grey?"

"Yeah. Just fine," I said, bracing myself for what was coming next.

"Heard you're leaving town today." She drilled her eyes into me.

I shrugged. "I hadn't planned it that way. But work, you know."

"I don't, actually." She leaned in closer, and the smell of White Diamonds filled the air. It was the same perfume my grandmother used to wear. Maybe she thought leaning in was somehow sterner. "I don't see how you can do it."

"Alice, try to understand. I have a whole career. I can't just do what I want." No matter what my heart said.

"I know you young ones don't like when the whole town gets in your business. But it's for your own good because you all have a lot to learn. Now, I've seen a lot more than you have, so I can say this with the utmost confidence." She bore her eyes into me. "You're about to make the biggest mistake of your life."

I huffed. "It's the Song of the Seasons Contest. It's a little dramatic to say missing it would be the biggest mistake of my life."

She pointed a finger in my face. "You know I'm not talking about the contest, Greyson Reeves. I'm talking about Chanel. This town has been waiting your whole lives to see you two get it together. When you finally figure it out, you ruin it."

Kes chuckled and polished off the last bite of his pie. He was having the time of his life watching me get lectured by the nosiest person in Cardwick.

"I tried to explain—"

Alice tapped the table. "She's not going to understand. As far as she's concerned, you let her down—for the second time."

"That wasn't my plan. This time it's not me that wants to end things with her," I said.

"It might as well be. You can't plan matters of the heart. I can only give you advice. But it's up to you what you do with it. If you lose her again, you'll never get her back." Her gaze was intense, and she made sure not to let up until my discomfort showed. Once it did, she shook her head and walked away.

You'll never get her back. That sentence was a weapon—one that was already threatening my oxygen supply. It was an impossible situation. I loved Chanel, but I had also built a life, one that was comfortable.

I glanced up at Kes, who shrugged.

"You're being no help." I was a little bitter that he'd just sat there, eating his pie, his head ping-ponging between Alice and me like he was watching a good tennis match.

"She delivered the motivational talk so I wouldn't have to."

"Can you be serious?"

Kes put his fork down and let his tattooed arm rest on the table. "We've been friends for a long time, so I feel like I can tell you the truth. As your friend, I don't think you really want to let Chanel go. You told her you weren't totally happy with your job. Now that you're back with her and you have a community obligation, you can't even tell said job that you'll get there on the original date? I think it's easy to run. You're panicking, man. Your equilibrium is changing, and you're afraid you're going to break things again. You're breaking them now so you don't have to worry about doing it later. The thing is, you don't even know that you'll do it. You're just afraid you will."

"You and those blasted self-help books," I said.

"But aren't you glad I read them?"

"No." I did my best to keep a straight face.

"No one can tell you what to do, but can you really live

without her?"

"I have for twelve years."

"I said live, not exist. Not the same."

But I was going to be on a plane in a few hours. Maybe *I was* running.

Chanel

I tried to get another practice session in this morning, but my head was all over the place. As I held my flute up to my lips, my fingers glided over the keys, but I stumbled through the notes. My pitch was off, and I couldn't seem to get it right. The music notes on the page blurred as I tried my best to focus. Everything was wrong, and there was no use. Music was usually able to save me. Would it this time?

I hated that Greyson could occupy so much space in my brain. I hated even more that I'd let my guard down. Now, I was going to have to live with the setback of my heart. And after all the work I'd done to forget about him. I'd have to figure out how to push it aside, because I had one more job to do before leaving Cardwick: to represent the town in the Song of the Seasons Contest.

You can do anything, Chanel. I kept repeating the phrase, just as I had done twelve years ago. It was my affirmation when things got tough.

Laughter from my family downstairs interrupted my thoughts. I looked at the time on my phone. It was time to start getting dressed for the performance. Greyson was probably headed to the airport now, if he wasn't already there. I'd done my hair and makeup, so I slipped on the sparkly red dress I'd ordered for today and headed downstairs.

Everyone was already dressed up in their fancy holiday attire. Mom, Auntie Franny, and Auntie Lyndie were taking a sister photo while Penny chatted with my other cousin, Halle. As my foot hit the last step, Halle spotted me and came running over.

"Chanel!" She threw her arms around me, and we held onto each other.

Penny hugged the both of us. "Reunited finally," she said.

We all laughed. "How was the flight, Professor Carter?" I asked Halle, adding an extra octave on the last two words so my voice would sound upbeat.

"Not bad. Christmas Eve isn't my favorite time to fly, but it was either that or I wasn't going to make it home. The curriculum deadlines they're imposing have been brutal. At least everything's set for next semester." She ran her fingers through her dark, wavy hair.

Penny studied me for a second and then lowered her voice. "You okay?"

I offered a slight smile. "I will be."

Penny threw an arm over my shoulder and squeezed. Halle did the same. So what if I didn't have Grey anymore? I had so much love right here.

"Is our star ready?" Mom called from where everyone was gathered near the tree.

"Now or never," I said as the three of us moved toward the front door. Everyone got up and did the same.

Auntie Franny took both my hands in hers. "I just want you to know that no matter what, we're all so proud of you."

"Yeah," Auntie Lyndie said. "Thanks for keeping our town traditions alive." She wrapped her arms around me and gave me a hug.

We got our coats, and we were out the door.

I pulled my coat tighter as I stared out the car window, watching Christmas lights and decorations melt into each other. While Mom and Dad chatted in the front seats, I went over our Christmas song a few times in my head, making sure I remembered how I wanted to phrase it and which parts I wanted to stand out more than others. I wasn't even nervous about it, but it did feel like something was missing. And it didn't matter that Grey was back on my quit list. I couldn't deny that I missed him, and this song wouldn't be the same without him.

"You're awfully quiet," Mom said, looking at me in the rearview mirror.

"Just got a lot on my mind right now," I said.

"Or maybe just one thing—or person?"

I rolled my eyes. "Mom, I know you wanted things to work out with me and Grey, but this just proves that we were never meant to be together. We were right to end things when we did."

"That's what you think this proves?" She let out a short, frustrated laugh. "Never known a more stubborn pair."

"Some things aren't meant to be."

She shook her head. "I know it's hard for you to trust again—especially Grey—but can you really say you did your part? A relationship is a two-way street."

"You think I'm to blame for him deciding to leave on the day we're supposed to perform?"

"Chanel. Darling, you have these perfect scenarios in your head for how things are supposed to go. But life is complicated. Put yourself in Grey's shoes. If he made you choose between him and your career, would you? Because that's what you're asking him to do."

I was quiet. My God, that was exactly what I was asking him to do. Though, I didn't think I meant to.

Dad cleared his throat and shifted in his seat. He was quiet, too, but I knew he agreed with Mom.

"He was supposed to sing this song with me, and we were going to—" But I couldn't finish that sentence because if I thought about our planned Christmas date, I wasn't going to be able to stop the flood that was already threatening to spill out of my eyes.

"It's okay to be disappointed, but I want you to think long and hard about the decision you're making to push Grey away. I think you two love each other."

I met her eyes in the mirror, my mouth hanging open.

"A mother knows these things."

"And a father," Dad chimed in.

Mom glanced in his direction and smiled. "You might get into another relationship and notice the same patterns. If you want to make something work, you're going to have to meet each other halfway. I'm not saying Grey is right. I'm not saying anyone's right. I'm just saying the two of you should be thinking a little more about compromise."

"It just all feels familiar," I mumbled, turning my attention back to the window.

"Yeah, and maybe that's what scares you. It's not that you think Grey is going to fail you again. It's that you remembered that he was the love of your life, and those feelings never really went away. I think, deep down, you both know those twelve years were a mistake. It's time to surrender."

That last sentence gutted me, but I didn't say anything else, and neither did my parents for the rest of the ride. I had been living these last twelve years denying what I felt, and I used my career to cover it up. I was proud of my accomplishments but doing it without Grey was a mistake.

When we were almost to Marvelwest, I pulled out my phone and typed a message out to Grey:

I'm sorry for overreacting. Couldn't let you leave without letting you know I don't want to stand in your way. I understand how important your career is to you. Good luck with the next leg of the tour, and have a safe flight.

Just as Dad was pulling into the parking spot, I put my phone on silent and dropped it into my purse. I didn't know what was in the cards for me and Grey, but Chanel Baldwin was ready to take the stage.

Greyson

"I just don't understand why you couldn't tell them you had another obligation here. I bet they would have understood." My mother folded her arms across her chest as I wheeled my suitcase down the driveway. Dad opened the trunk, and I lifted it in.

"Mom, we've been over this a million times. I have responsibilities—ones that pay my bills."

"Don't worry about it, son. We get it. Your mom's just disappointed you're not going to be home for Christmas after all. She was looking forward to spending it with you—we both were."

"I know. I'm disappointed, too. But I have a job to do. And I'd rather not stand out here in the cold, arguing with both of you."

Mom shook her head, and it reminded me of all the times she did so when I messed up as a kid.

We all got in the car, each of our doors slamming shut. Dad eased the car back, and I tried to ignore the mix of guilt and regret pressing against my lungs.

I tried to soften the moment. "Can't you look at it for what it is? We still got time together." I touched Mom's shoulder from the backseat.

She patted my hand. "If you change your mind right now, we can still make it over to Marvelwest."

"Mom."

She didn't say anything else. Instead, she let out a heavy sigh. I guess I couldn't blame her for being upset. I was angry at myself, too.

I'd let everyone down—especially Chanel. It was the last thing I wanted. Yet, here I was, doing it anyway. I was trying to have my cake and eat it, too, as my mother would tell me growing up. My phone buzzed in my pocket. When I pulled it out, my heart lurched in my chest against my will when I read the name on the screen. I swiped my thumb across it so quickly I almost dropped the phone. My pulse surged as I read her text, then I just felt like an even bigger jerk for leaving.

I read her words over and over while I tried to process my

thoughts. I pictured getting to the airport. I pictured checking in, waiting at the gate, and getting on that plane. I pictured Chanel stepping onstage, ready to blow everyone away, but without me. I pictured us going about our respective careers over the next few years, but separately. And then I pictured my life the way it'd been for twelve years alone and the way it'd been over the last few days in Cardwick with her. And last, I pictured my future self with Chanel by my side.

There was no contest.

I'd gotten a second taste of what it was like to have her. And I'd scratched the record. It was just as Alice had said: it was about to be the biggest mistake of my life—make that the second biggest. I wouldn't make it without her. All this time, I'd been homesick, but not for a place. Chanel was my home. She always had been.

I tugged at the neckline of my sweater and shifted in my seat. Mom turned her head to look at me. "You okay, Grey? You look like you're about to pass out."

"Should I pull over?" Dad asked.

I finally had the guts to say, "No. You should do a one-eighty."

Chanel

ackstage at the Marvelwest Auditorium, I gave myself a final once-over in the mirror. The dressing room they gave me was alive with Christmas decorations, which didn't do much for my mood, though I wished it would. I touched the branches on the tiny tree they had on the vanity. Real needles landed next to where I'd put down my purse. I was on next, second from the top. At least I wasn't first.

The host's voice echoed through the thin walls. "We are so happy you all could make it out to the annual Song of the Seasons Contest." Cheers and clapping erupted from the audience.

I was ready for this, but I still felt this unshakeable gloom. I opened one of the bottles of water that the volunteers had left for the performers and gulped it down, wishing it would wash away whatever I was feeling.

The door to the dressing room opened, and a teenage girl with red-orange hair and turquoise glasses poked her head in. "Ms. Baldwin?"

I spun to face her. "Yes, come in."

"Hi, I'm Amber. We've got about five minutes. You all set?"

I let out a deep breath. "Yeah."

I followed her out to the spot behind a beautiful velvet curtain where I'd be exchanging places with the current act onstage. Marvelwest had an impressive auditorium. About a year ago they'd upgraded everything with a modern design and updated technology.

Amber looked at the clipboard she carried and adjusted her glasses. "Okay. I see there was a change to your performance. Cool. You can just wait here. Once this act is done, the hosts will come to the stage again, say a few things, and introduce you, okay?"

"Sounds great," I said.

Amber patted me on the shoulder, and I couldn't tell if she was genuinely cheering me on or offering me pity. "Good luck out there, Ms. Baldwin."

I smiled. "Thanks."

Just as the trio performing finished up, the host came onto

the stage. "Wasn't that a beautiful song? The talent tonight is going all out! Our judges are going to have their work cut out for them!"

The audience clapped.

"Now, our next act is a song written by two of Cardwick's very best. These two have had impressive careers in the classical music realm. Although today's song was written by both Chanel Baldwin and Greyson Reeves, we regret to let everyone know that Greyson couldn't be here tonight."

My heart took a dive hearing those words. *Stay focused, Chanel.*

"Such is the life of a renowned conductor!"

The crowd cheered.

"Although we'll miss Greyson, we're thrilled to have Chanel, a highly regarded flutist in her own right. Singing 'The Christmas I Found You,' please welcome Chanel Baldwin!"

Time to turn on.

I stepped out on the stage, waving as I made my way to the center where the piano waited for me. The bright lights felt hot against my skin already. Maybe it was the adrenaline. I took a seat and adjusted the mic.

"Thank you all for being here tonight. The Song of the Seasons Contest has always been one of my favorites growing up, and I'm so glad I made it home this year to perform for you."

More cheering.

I straightened my back, my fingers hovering over the keys. Once I took a deep breath, my fingers pressed down on the keys, gliding across them all as I played the melody Grey and I wrote. I closed my eyes and sang the first line.

"Almost Christmas and the fire's burning bright."

When I got to the next line where Grey was supposed to sing, a smooth and dangerously sweet voice filled the air alongside mine.

"It's just me and you on this cold winter night."

My eyes flew open, and the audience gasped, then clapped as Grey walked to the center of the stage. My heart stumbled in my chest, and I almost forgot the words I was supposed to be singing.

He finally reached the piano, and when he looked at me, it ignited a fire through my whole body. He sat next to me, and we sang the rest of our song, just as we had planned. The audience clapped when it ended, but Grey and I stared at each other, that fire raging stronger than ever between us.

He leaned down so close that his lips touched just enough of my ear to make me shiver, and he whispered, "You look beautiful, but we better get offstage before people get a show they didn't sign up for."

My stomach clenched, as was often the case when I was in close proximity to him. He stood up and reached for my hand. We both turned to face the audience, taking a bow as the energy in the room exploded. We exited and made our way backstage.

Grey didn't let go of my hand.

"Weren't you supposed to be on a plane?" I asked.

He took both my hands in his and kissed the backs of them.

It sent my heart on a speed mission, but it made me want to cry, too.

He stared into my eyes. "I was. But things change."

"What things?"

"I thought I was going to come back here, and I'd see you, and I'd maybe feel nostalgic. I was convinced we'd both moved on. Twelve years is enough time for people to forget each other. We were supposed to leave here and go our separate ways again."

I cracked a smile. "And you were supposed to be on my quit list."

He smiled that same boyish smile that made me fall in love with him right from the start. "Ever since I've been back in Cardwick, there's been a song in my heart. And I'm not talking about the music we've been making together. It's you, babe. You are the song in my heart. You give me everything I didn't know I needed."

"Grey."

I closed the space between us, and his hands cupped the sides of my face. I wrapped my arms around his waist, and he said, "You breathe life back into everything—into Christmas, into this town, into my heart...into me. I love you, Chanel Baldwin."

"I love you, too, Greyson Reeves."

His lips covered mine, and all I wanted was this man. I was never going to let him go again.

He pulled away slowly and wrapped his arms around me.

"Was your boss mad?" I asked.

He shrugged. "Don't know."

"Wait, what?"

"I haven't said anything. It's just a job. I'd rather lose a job than my person." He grinned. "Besides, maybe it's time to get to work on that music school."

I studied his face. "That would be a big change."

"Someone once called me out for being afraid of change. Thought I might give it a try."

I touched the side of his face. "So, does this mean I still have a Christmas date?"

He twisted his mouth and pretended he was thinking hard. "That depends."

My mouth hung open in a playful way. "Depends on what?"

"Depends on if I'm off your quit list."

We both laughed. "Only if you promise me that the rest of your Christmases are mine."

He held me tighter. "Forever."

Epilogue
One year later
Grayson

*C*hanel was going to be heading over to her parents' house any minute now. I had just finished hanging the lights on the gazebo her father built over the summer. Mrs. Baldwin was running a garland she made of poinsettias, pine, and various gold Christmas-themed trinkets along the railing. I grabbed the special wreath that Alice had made and hung it at the top of the entry point of the gazebo. I took a step back and folded my arms over my chest. It was perfect. I was getting more nervous as the minutes ticked by, and despite the cold weather, I was ready to throw myself in the lake to keep my body temperature from continuing to rise.

Mr. Baldwin clapped me on the back and took a sip of hot chocolate from his "Dad Knows Best" mug. "Don't look so worried. She's going to love it."

"I hope you're right." I prayed my voice didn't waver too much.

He held up the mug and pointed, then raised an eyebrow.

We both laughed. "Good point," I said.

He gazed out at the gazebo. "Everything's going to turn out just fine."

I kept my eyes forward. "Thanks for lightening the mood... and giving me permission to marry your daughter."

He reached out his hand to shake mine. "We've known you were the one since the first day you came over to do homework with Chanel." He winked.

"That long, huh?"

He chuckled. "I think you knew, too. Don't forget to turn on the outdoor heater I installed."

As if I'd need it.

He took another sip from his cup and walked back inside to join the rest of Chanel's family and my parents. I knew Chanel would want everyone here. I also invited Harley and

Kes, because my boys had been there this whole time, rooting for us, even if I was too stupid to get it.

I grabbed my suit jacket from the railing and exchanged it with the heavier coat I was wearing. I patted the inner pocket to make sure the ornament Chanel gave me was still there. I'd always been glad it was a little smaller than the size of a typical ornament, but I was especially thankful today. It was all part of the plan.

Mrs. Baldwin backed away from the gazebo after she finished decorating and took it in. She gave a slight nod, like she was proud of her work. The garland took the lighted gazebo to the next level. It was romantic against the backdrop of the lake, and I couldn't wait for Chanel to see it.

Mrs. Baldwin beamed. "You did well, Grey."

I pointed to her and then myself. "We did well."

She gave me a hug. "I'm going to go inside and make sure everyone's tucked away so Chanel doesn't see them when she comes in."

"Thank you," I said. It was all I could manage to get out. My heart and my thoughts were in the most competitive race.

"Breathe, Grey," she said over her shoulder as she made her way back to the porch.

I took her advice and let out a deep exhale, my breath like smoke floating through the frigid cold. I paced the gazebo back and forth, praying it might quell my nerves. I'd wanted to do this when we officially got back together last year, but

I also recognized Chanel needed time to get used to us being together again. Plus, I needed to finish up the last leg of the tour, and she was starting that new job as music director at Marvelwest. There was just too much readjusting. But now, things had settled, and I couldn't wait a second longer.

The porch door swung open. I didn't even have to turn around to know it was her. I could always feel when her heart was close.

"Grey? What's—"

When I turned to face her, she was staring out at the gazebo.

"Who did that? It's gorgeous," she said.

"It's for you," I said, walking out to meet her where she was at the screen door.

"What are you up to, Greyson Reeves?"

I smirked. "Why do you always think I'm up to something?"

She smacked my arm playfully. "Because you are."

"Come with me," I said.

I opened the door and caught her scent. Vanilla and roses. It always made me dizzy, so I had to work extra hard to keep my focus. I took her hand and walked with her back toward the gazebo.

Once we stepped onto the gazebo, I said, "The gazebo is new, but this lake isn't."

"No, it's not," she said.

I shifted my gaze back to the porch. "Your parents' porch was practically my second home."

She laughed. "Yeah. They would joke about it, too. You were always here."

"That's right. I was always here," I said, this time staring into her eyes. I'd done it so many times before, but it was never enough. I wanted more of this, and I wanted it forever.

I cleared my throat and held both of her hands.

Her family all came out then. Chanel glanced over to the porch, her brows furrowing. I let go of her hand, reached into my pocket, and pulled out the ornament she'd given me.

"Recognize this?" I asked, holding the ceramic ornament in my palm.

Her eyes widened. "You kept it? All these years? Grey…"

"How could I get rid of my lucky ornament? It's been my good luck charm for every single concert," I said.

"I can't believe you kept that ancient thing." She laughed.

I took my time opening it, and she gasped. She placed one hand over her mouth and one over her heart.

I dropped to one knee. "I wish I could take back those years we spent apart. I wish we could somehow get them back. Sadly, time machines don't exist. That's out of our control now, but we can control how we move forward. And I want you to be part of all my seconds. I love you, Chanel. And I would be honored if you would spend the rest of your life with me. Will you marry me?" My heart had been moving at allegro all day, but now I wouldn't be the least bit surprised if it burst right through my chest.

A tear slipped from Chanel's eyes, which said a lot because she didn't like people to see her cry.

She nodded her head up and down. "Yes, Grey, I'd love to be your wife."

Finally, I felt lighter. Cheers erupted from the porch, and as I stood up, Chanel threw her arms around my neck, her lips crashing into mine. Remembering we had an audience, we pulled away, and I whispered, "To be continued." She smiled as I placed the ring on her left ring finger.

Our family and friends came running to the gazebo to give us hugs and offer us congratulations. While we chatted, I noticed Alice whispering and laughing with our moms and Chanel's aunts. I shook my head. Chanel and I had both suspected they were up to something, but they'd never admit it. Whatever they were talking about, they sure were getting a kick out of it.

Once things had calmed down some, Mrs. Baldwin said, "This is the best Christmas season ever! I made a big pot of pelau and some ponche de crème. Come, let's have a good time."

The crowd started to make their way inside. Chanel and I hung back, and I grabbed her hand.

"I guess this means I *truly* have to retire that quit list, huh?" she said.

I laughed. "Let's be real, was I ever really on that list?" I raised an eyebrow.

But she just smiled, placed a hand on my cheek, and kissed me instead.

I love hearing from my readers and seeing photos of them enjoying my books online!

Tag me in your photos on
Instagram: @racquelhenry
Twitter: @racquelhenry
Facebook: RacquelHenryAuthor
TikTok: @therealracquelhenry

If you liked the two lines from the song Grey and Chanel wrote, listen to an exclusive soundbite by signing up for my newsletter! You'll also be able to stay up to date on new releases and writing news! Sign up here: racquelhenry.com/CardwickExtras.

Ready for the next books in the Cardwick series? Be sure that you're signed up for my newsletter for exclusive first looks and release dates!

Also By Racquel Henry

Find out more about Racquel and sign up for her
newsletter at www.racquelhenry.com
Find more publications at
https://racquelhenry.com/publications/

About the Author

Racquel Henry is a Trinidadian writer, editor, and writing coach with an MFA from Fairleigh Dickinson University. She spent six years as an English Professor and currently owns the writing studio, Writer's Atelier, in Maitland, FL. In 2010, Racquel co-founded Black Fox Literary Magazine where she still serves as an editor, and recently joined Voyage YA Journal as Editor-in-Chief. Since 2013, Racquel has presented and moderated panels at writing conferences, residencies, and private writing groups across the US. She is the author of Holiday on Park, Letter to Santa, and The Writer's Atelier Little Book of Writing Affirmations. Her script, Christmas Magic at Holly Oaks, is currently optioned with Rom Com Pictures. Racquel's fiction, poetry, and nonfiction has appeared in Lotus-Eater Magazine, Reaching Beyond the Saguaros: A Collaborative Prosimetric Travelogue (Serving House Books, 2017), We Can't Help it if We're From Florida (Burrow Press, 2017), Moko Caribbean Arts & Letters, among others. When she's not writing, editing, or coaching writers, you can find her watching Hallmark Christmas movies.

15609043R00075